ABT

ACPL I

DISCARDED

P9-BIV-051

1/05

Violet's Perplexing Puzzles

Violet's Perplexing Puzzles

BOOK FIVE

of the
A Life of Faith:
Violet Travilla
Series

Based on the characters by
Martha Finley

MCP
Mission City Press
Franklin, Tennessee

Book Five of the *A Life of Faith: Violet Travilla* Series

Violet's Perplexing Puzzles
Copyright © 2005, Mission City Press, Inc. All Rights Reserved.

Published by Mission City Press, Inc.

This book is based on the *Elsie Dinsmore* series written by Martha Finley and first published in 1868 by Dodd, Mead & Company.

Cover & Interior Design: Richmond & Williams
Cover Photography: Michelle Grisco Photography
Typesetting: BookSetters

Unless otherwise indicated, all Scripture references are from the Holy Bible, New International Version (NIV). Copyright © 1973, 1978, 1984 by International Bible Society. Used by permission of Zondervan Publishing House, Grand Rapids, MI. All rights reserved.

For more information, write to Mission City Press at 202 Second Avenue South, Franklin, Tennessee 37064, or visit our Web Site at:

www.alifeoffaith.com

Library of Congress Catalog Card Number: 2004106103
Finley, Martha
  Violet's Perplexing Puzzles
  Book Five of the *A Life of Faith: Violet Travilla* Series
  ISBN: 1-928749-21-6

Printed in the United States of America
1 2 3 4 5 6 7 8 — 10 09 08 07 06 05

— FOREWORD —

*V*i Travilla seems to have found her life's work: service to the Lord through service to others. In *Violet's Bold Mission* — the previous volume in the *A Life of Faith: Violet Travilla* series — she moved to India Bay and established a mission in the city's poorest district. But not everything went as Vi expected, and she learned that helping others can sometimes require personal courage as well as good will. In *Violet's Perplexing Puzzles*, she and the other residents at Samaritan House will face more dilemmas that test their commitment, and Vi's dedication to the mission will soon become entangled with new emotions.

Drawing on characters and situations created by Martha Finley in the nineteenth century, the Violet Travilla series continues the saga of the Dinsmore and Travilla families that first enchanted and inspired readers more that 130 years ago. In the spirit of Miss Finley's original novels, these new versions are intended to inspire young Christians of today. The story of Vi, her family, and friends reflects the timeless values and principles that were the foundation of all Miss Finley's writings and remain the bedrock of Christian faith and practice in the twenty-first century.

Mission City Press is pleased to present this latest installment in the series and to continue the story of Vi's determination to live Christ's commandment by serving those less fortunate than herself.

Violet's Perplexing Puzzles

∾ SETTLEMENT HOUSES AND THE SPIRIT OF CHRIST ∾

If Vi Travilla had been a real person, she would have been a pioneer. Samaritan House, her mission in the fictional Southern city of India Bay, might have been called a *settlement house* or *neighborhood house* — a place inside a poor community where volunteers lived and offered a variety of services to their neighbors.

In our story, the recipients of Samaritan House are primarily poor white people, as segregation in the South was the norm, and whites and blacks did not live in the same neighborhoods.

The first settlement house was founded in London in 1884. A vicar in the Church of England, Reverend Samuel A. Barnett, his wife, and several university students "settled" in a house, called Toynbee Hall, in an impoverished part of the city. Reverend Barnett's idea was to live in the community in order to understand the real needs of the people there.

The work at Toynbee Hall inspired Americans Charles B. Stover and Stanton Colt to establish a settlement house in New York City in 1886. The most famous settlement in the U.S. was Hull House, opened in Chicago in 1889 by Jane Addams and Ellen Gates Starr. That same year, another settlement was started in New York City by Jane Robbins and Jean Fine Spahr.

The early settlements were residential centers based on a commitment to equality among the people who served and the people of the community. These settlements were usually not associated with a specific religion, though their principles often reflected the Christian beliefs of their founders.

Foreword

Jane Addams wrote that her goal for Hull House was "to share the lives of the poor" and to serve others in ways that would "express the spirit of Christ."

The settlement movement is credited with many developments that remain a part of our culture, including the first youth groups and special services for senior citizens. Participants in the movement were active in efforts to enact laws to protect the poor and disenfranchised, including child labor laws and the establishment of juvenile courts, workmen's compensation for job-related injuries and disabilities, regulation of workplace hours and safety measures, and pensions for widowed mothers. Most American settlements provided education, such as English language classes for immigrants, training for people who needed new job skills, and even college-level courses. They sponsored athletic teams and hobby groups, and settlements often included cultural activities—music and arts—and free libraries.

Settlements tended to attract bright, idealistic, well-educated, young volunteer workers. They took what they learned back to their colleges and universities, and a new area of education emerged: social science, and particularly social work. A number of the nation's most effective reformers got their start in settlement houses—like Frances Perkins, who worked at Hull House during her college years and later became the first woman appointed to a U.S. President's cabinet (Secretary of Labor, 1933-1945).

Related to the settlement movement were groups including "good government" organizations, which sought to root out corruption in local governments; promoters of free, public education for all children; and adherents to the "social gospel," a movement among American Christians to

apply Christ's teachings about charity and justice to reform of the country's social and labor systems. Progress could be slow, but by World War I (1914-1918), much was being learned about the real causes of poverty, and many reforms were underway.

∽ JANE ADDAMS ∽

When people today speak of "social work," the name of Jane Addams is often mentioned first. Hull House set standards that still influence the ways that social and community services are provided. Her work with the poor, and later in the cause of peace, brought international respect and fame, and in 1931, she became only the second woman to receive the Nobel Peace Prize.

For young people today, it can be heartening to learn about her early years. Jane Addams struggled to discover her purpose in life and was almost thirty years old before she finally found her path to service.

Laura Jane Addams—born in the small town of Cedarville, Illinois, on September 6, 1860—was the eighth of nine children. Her father, John Addams, was a Quaker and a prosperous businessman, owning both a flour and a saw mill; he was also a director of a bank and a railroad. He served in the Illinois State Legislature for almost two decades and was a friend of President Abraham Lincoln.

Jane's mother, Sarah, was a strong-willed and capable woman who often ran her husband's mills when he was away. But Sarah died when Jane was only three, and young "Jenny," as Jane was called by her family, was raised without much discipline or attention to the social graces.

She was very close to her father and credited him with introducing her to "the moral concerns of life." In her auto-biography, Jane remembered her first encounter with the kind of poverty that would become her life's work. She was about seven years old, and she accompanied her father to a mill in the poorest section of a neighboring town. Jane wondered "why people lived in such horrid little houses so close together." After her father explained, Jane declared that when she grew up, she would live in a "large house…right in the midst of the horrid little houses…."

Jane suffered from a curvature of the spine, which affected her self-confidence. She was shy among people she didn't know, and for some time, she was hesitant to be seen with her father at church, fearful that strangers might think less of him because of his daughter. Though people who knew her said she was a pretty child, Jane described herself as "the ugly, pigeon-toed little girl, whose crooked back obliged her to walk with her head held very much upon one side…."

Still, she seems never to have been afraid to turn to her revered father for guidance. Once, when she asked him about a difficult theological concept, he told her that it was probably beyond their understanding. Then he said "that it was very important not to pretend to understand what you didn't understand and that you must always be honest with yourself inside, whatever happened." It was a lesson Jane never forgot.

When Jane was eight, her father remarried. His second wife, Anna Halderman Addams, had two sons, and the younger became Jane's playmate and good friend. She didn't always get along with her stepmother, but from

Anna, Jane learned aspects of self-discipline and good manners that later served her well in her public career.

Jane attended the local public school until she was seventeen. Then, like her older sisters, she entered Rockford Female Seminary (later Rockford College for Women), a boarding college of which her father was a trustee. Her special interest was history, and she also read widely in literature and studied several languages. An excellent student, she graduated at the top of her class. Jane and her friends, "ardent girls, who discussed everything under the sun with unabated interest," were serious about the opportunities that education offered. Among her close friends, one became a missionary teacher in Japan, one became a medical missionary in Korea, another was a gifted teacher of the blind, and one was a librarian in the forefront of the effort to open libraries for everyone.

At Rockford, Jane experienced a good deal of pressure to enter the missionary field. Despite her idealism, she resisted. By the end of her senior year, she had decided that she would study medicine and "live with the poor." But her plans were vague, and the next eight years did not go as she imagined.

After a winter studying at the Women's Medical College in Philadelphia, she left to have surgery on her spine and endured six months of recovery "literally bound to a bed...." She was then sent to Europe for two years to recuperate and regain her strength. Early in her travels, she was among a group touring London's impoverished East End, guided by a city missionary. There she witnessed a midnight auction sale of rotting vegetables and fruits. Jane later wrote of the desperately poor bidders and their "hands, empty, pathetic, nerveless and workworn, showing

white in the uncertain light of the street, and clutching forward for food which was already unfit to eat."

From this time, she was "irresistibly drawn to the poorer districts" of each European city she visited. Her distress was heightened by her sense that there were no answers in her middle-class background. She felt alone and helpless, and she resented that her education hadn't prepared her for "the bitter poverty and the social maladjustment which is all about...."

Returning to Cedarville, she joined the Presbyterian church, in part because something made her "long for an outward symbol of fellowship, some bond of peace, some blessed spot where unity of spirit might claim right of way over all differences." She traveled in the U.S. and saw the conditions of the poor in her homeland. Her "dedication to the ideals of democracy" led her to deeper questions about the separation of the privileged few and the many who lived in ignorance and poverty. She went through several years of depression as she struggled to know what she — a young single woman from a prosperous family, well educated but rather frail physically — could do to help.

During a second trip to Europe, Jane began to form a plan for a settlement house "in which young women who had been given over too exclusively to study might restore a balance of activity...and learn of life from life itself...." In 1888, she visited Toynbee Hall in London. She was twenty-eight years old, and after many arduous years of searching, she had at last found her direction.

Returning to Illinois, Jane and her college friend Ellen Starr rented an old mansion, named Hull House for its original owner, in one of Chicago's working-class, immigrant neighborhoods. Jane, Ellen, and their housekeeper, Mary

Keyser, moved there in September 18, 1889. Their mission, stated in the Hull House charter, was "to provide a center for a higher civic and social life; to institute and maintain educational and philanthropic enterprises; and to investigate and improve the conditions in the industrial sections of Chicago."

Volunteers, including young women from backgrounds similar to Jane's, soon joined the founders. They organized a kindergarten, a daycare center, children's clubs, evening classes for young people no longer able to attend school, and outreach programs for the elderly. Jane wrote, "We were asked to wash the new-born babies, and to prepare the dead for burial, and to 'mind the children.' " Bonds were forged among the residents, volunteers, and their neighbors. In Jane's words, "These first days laid the simple human foundations," which would underlie all the work of Hull House.

By its third year, Hull House was serving more than 2,000 people every week. Eventually its facilities were expanded to thirteen buildings, including a community kitchen, a gymnasium and swimming pool, an art gallery, and a bookbindery. It offered employment services and also became a major training center for social workers.

Through her work at Hull House, Jane became an ardent advocate for reform in laws related to the welfare of children, the rights of working people and immigrants, and women's suffrage. Small in stature and feminine in manner, Jane was imbued with extraordinary energy and determination — even when her work led to controversy and personal attacks. (At one time, she was called the most dangerous woman in America.) Foreseeing the coming of World War I, she became a tireless crusader for peace, serving as chairperson of the Women's Peace Party in the

Foreword

U.S. and president of the Women's International League for Peace and Freedom.

Jane died in 1935, but not before seeing many of the reforms she fought for become reality. Her funeral was held at Hull House; then thousands of mourners gathered along the railroad tracks to pay tribute as a train bore her body to Cedarville for burial—back to the place where she had learned the principles that guided her work in service to the greater good of society.

In her lifetime, she received countless awards and honors, but her life itself remains her highest accolade. For almost thirty years, she struggled to find her way. For the next forty-five years, she gave herself totally and joyfully to rekindling the humanitarian spirit of the early Christians—a "new treasure" that found its expression in following Jesus' commandment to love all people without distinction or reservation.

Readers interested in learning more about Jane Addams might begin with her 1910 autobiography, *Twenty Years at Hull-House*, which is available in paperback editions. A follow-up book, *The Second Twenty Years at Hull-House*, was published in 1930. Biographies of Miss Addams, including books for young readers, can be found in most local libraries.

xiii

TRAVILLA/DINSMORE FAMILY TREE

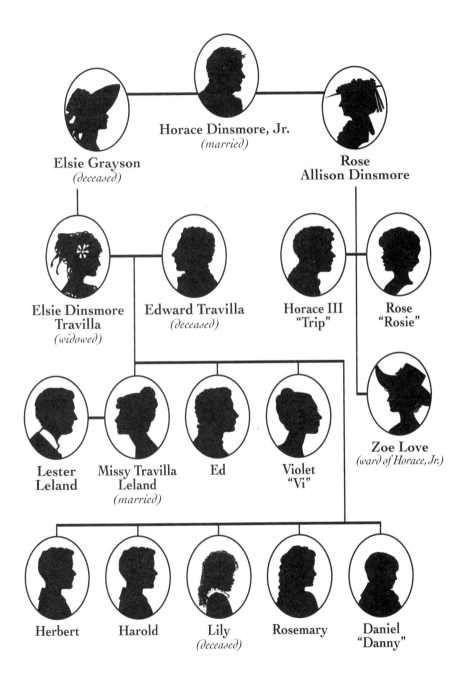

Horace Dinsmore, Jr.
(married)

Elsie Grayson
(deceased)

Rose
Allison Dinsmore

Elsie Dinsmore
Travilla
(widowed)

Edward Travilla
(deceased)

Horace III
"Trip"

Rose
"Rosie"

Lester
Leland

Missy Travilla
Leland
(married)

Ed

Violet
"Vi"

Zoe Love
(ward of Horace, Jr.)

Herbert

Harold

Lily
(deceased)

Rosemary

Daniel
"Danny"

SETTING

$\mathscr{T}$he story opens at Samaritan House, a mission in the Wildwood district of the Southern seaport city of India Bay. It is December 1883.

CHARACTERS

Violet Travilla (Vi), age 20, the third child of Elsie and the late Edward Travilla; founder of Samaritan House

Elsie Dinsmore Travilla, Vi's mother; a wealthy widow; owner of Ion and other properties in the South

Edward Travilla, Jr. (Ed), age 24, Vi's older brother; a university graduate

(Vi's younger brothers and sister are **Herbert** and **Harold**, twins, age 17; **Rosemary**, age 13; and **Danny**, age 9. Vi's elder sister, **Missy Leland**, lives in Rome, Italy, with her artist husband, **Lester**.)

Mrs. Maurene O'Flaherty, Vi's companion and friend; resident of Samaritan House

Ben and **Crystal Johnson**, long-time household servants at Ion

Aunt Chloe, revered nursemaid and friend to Elsie Travilla and her children

Horace Dinsmore, Jr. and his wife, **Rose**, Vi's grandparents; owners of The Oaks plantation

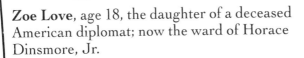

Zoe Love, age 18, the daughter of a deceased American diplomat; now the ward of Horace Dinsmore, Jr.

Adelaide Dinsmore Allison, Vi's great-aunt who lives in Philadelphia with her husband, **Edward**, a wealthy industrialist

∞ INDIA BAY ∞

Dr. Silas Lansing, an eminent surgeon, and his wife, **Naomi**, prominent citizens of India Bay

Enoch and Christine Reeve, caretaker and house-keeper at Samaritan House, and their toddler son, **Jacob**

Miss Emily Clayton, Samaritan House clinic nurse

Dr. David Bowman, a physician and volunteer at Samaritan House

Mrs. Mary Appleton, cook at Samaritan House, and her daughter, **Polly**, age 6

Tansy Evans, age 11, and **Marigold Evans**, age 6, orphaned sisters who live at Samaritan House

Dr. Marcus Darius Raymond, a university profes-sor and friend of the Travilla family; a widower with three children

Seth Fredericks, a schoolteacher

Mr. Williams, a pastor in Boxtown

Reverend and **Mrs. Stephens**, minister of a Wildwood church, and his wife

Alma Hansen, an immigrant from Germany

Tobias Clinch, owner of the Wildwood Hotel

Widow Amos, **Miss Bessie Moran**, **Mrs. Lamar**, and other residents of Wildwood

Mr. Archibald, a master carpenter

Oscar and **Ethel Evans** and **Mrs. Idanell Granger**, elderly Pennsylvania residents

CHAPTER

1

News of Sadness and Cheer

Therefore encourage each other with these words.

1 THESSALONIANS 4:18

*T*he mood of the residents of Samaritan House had been subdued. In the gentlest way, the ladies of the mission had told young Tansy and Marigold Evans of the death of their mother, and to the best of everyone's ability, the children were comforted in their grief.

The girls never doubted that their mother had gone to be with God. They rejoiced that she was in His Heaven where there is no pain and suffering and that she was waiting for them there. But the girls felt her loss deeply. They would not see their "Mommy" again in this life or hear her sweet voice or feel her loving embrace. All hope of an earthly reunion was gone, and as far as anyone knew, the girls were alone in the world.

"Are we orphans now?" Marigold, who was approaching her sixth birthday, asked Vi one evening several days after the children had learned the truth.

Vi Travilla and her dear friend Zoe Love, who was staying at the mission for several weeks, were sitting at the kitchen table with the little girls. They had finished their supper, and Mrs. O'Flaherty, Vi's invaluable companion, was putting away the last of the clean dishes. Mary Appleton, the mission's cook, was checking the supplies in the pantry, and her daughter, Polly, had just climbed onto the chair next to Marigold's.

Vi looked into Marigold's eyes and was glad to see that there were no tears.

"Yes," Vi said calmly, "you are orphans in the strict sense. But I don't like the word because it sounds so harsh. Your mother and father and grandmother have gone to God, but you will always have their love in your hearts. You'll never forget how much they loved you."

"That's true," Zoe added. "I'm an orphan, too. My mother died when I was younger than you, Marigold, and my Papa died when I was sixteen. But I know they are with me still, in here"—she laid her hand over her heart—"and that in Heaven, they love me as they always did. So I don't think of myself as orphaned, because I still have their love and the love of my Heavenly Father."

They were all silent for some moments. The large old house, which was now a mission for the poor and helpless people of the Wildwood neighborhood in the seaport city of India Bay, bustled with activity during the day. But in the dark of a December evening, it was very still.

Young Polly, who was just a few months older than Marigold, put her small hand on her friend's shoulder. Softly, she said, "Jesus loves you and Tansy. He doesn't want you to be sad."

Marigold smiled at her friend and said, "I know, Polly. I always know that. And Mommy's happy in Heaven with Him."

After that night, the Evans girls began to talk more freely about their mother and their old lives in South Carolina. As time passed, the children's sadness began to lift. Whatever was to come next for them, the girls decided, Jesus had put them in Miss Vi's hands, and they would be safe.

Meanwhile, Vi was doing what she could to assure the girls' future. The children were heiresses now—having inherited a valuable farm in South Carolina. It had come to them from the estate of a kind woman, Mrs. Greer, who had owned a large plantation and—in the days before the end of slavery—the girls' mother and grandmother.

After a frightening incident, when Mrs. Greer's despicable son had attempted to kidnap Tansy and Marigold in order to get control of their property, the residents of Samaritan House kept a close guard on the girls. But there had been no more threats to the children. A series of strange occurrences, including a cruel attack on the mission's pet cat and an unexplained fire in the storage shed, also seemed to have ended. At the mission, they suspected that all these events could be traced to Mr. Tobias Clinch, the owner of the Wildwood Hotel and saloon, but there was no evidence of his involvement. Mr. Greer and the leader of the would-be kidnappers had escaped India Bay and left the state. Gradually, a sense of relief replaced the anxious feelings at the mission. The residents became hopeful that such dangers were behind them and that they could focus their minds on the future of their two precious orphans.

For the time being, Vi's mother, Elsie Travilla, was acting as legal guardian for the children. But before any plans could be made, they had to find out if the Evans girls had other relatives. This question was now under investigation by Vi's great-aunt and great-uncle in Pennsylvania. Every day, Vi searched the mail for news from her Aunt Adelaide Allison, but there was no word until shortly before Christmas.

It was after breakfast, and Vi had gone to her office. She happened to notice the little calendar on her desk. Tuesday, December 18—one more week until their first Christmas at the mission.

Enoch Reeve, the caretaker at Samaritan House, brought in the mail, but before reading the letters, Vi reviewed the day's tasks with Enoch. He reported on their supplies of coal, hay, and horse feed, and he mentioned some repairs he needed to make. As he went through his list of chores, Vi had a sudden thought: *We truly are a working mission now. Samaritan House isn't just a dream anymore. The people of Wildwood are accepting us as friends and neighbors, and we've had no more trouble from those who wanted to frighten us away. Thank You, Lord, for blessing our efforts and guiding us through our time of strife.*

After Enoch left, Vi remembered the stack of letters. She expected only business correspondence, but on the top of the pile lay a cream-colored envelope addressed in a hand-writing that Vi instantly recognized. It was from her Aunt Adelaide in Philadelphia.

Vi opened the envelope and hurriedly located her spectacles under some papers on the desk. She put them on and read the letter.

Dearest Niece,

Your Uncle Edward and I believe we have located the grandparents of your young friends! It will require more time to confirm the information, so I think you should withhold it from the children for now. I would not want to raise their hopes until we are sure. But the news is hopeful. After a lengthy search of the records, our investigator uncovered the registration of the birth of a John Evans who matches the few details you were able to discover about the children's father. The investigator has now traced the Evans family to a small town in northeastern Pennsylvania. He will go there between Christmas and New Year's Day to determine if they are the family you seek. I pray to our dear Lord that they are. Your letter explaining the girls' position now that their mother is gone touched all of us deeply.

What brave children they are, and how deserving, after their trials, of being united with their father's parents.

Vi quickly scanned the rest of the letter, which was about the latest doings of the Allisons and their children and grandchildren. Then she went back and read the opening paragraph again.

Oh, how I wish I could share this with the girls, she thought, *but Aunt Adelaide is right. It would be wrong to raise false hopes. If it is Your will, Lord, please let my aunt's next report be good. Grant our dear Tansy and Marigold the gift of a loving family. But if that is not to be, bless them with Your love and help them hold firm to the faith that has sustained them through so much loss and sorrow. Help us, too, Lord, to support and guide these wonderful children as they go forward on the path You have set for them, wherever it may lead.*

Vi then went back to her other mail, and it was what she expected—bills and business matters. But the last letter was something else. Her name and address had been written in a bold hand, and the postmark was "Boston." There were several sheets in the envelope, and she turned to the last page.

Though the office was comfortably warm, Vi shivered unconsciously when she saw the signature. She turned back to the first page and began to read:

Dear Miss Travilla,

I apologize for my delay in writing to thank you for your hospitality during my last visit to India Bay. Your mother and your entire family showed me such kindness during my sojourn in the South. I particularly wanted to tell you how impressed I was by your speech at Dr. and Mrs. Lansing's ball. Cold indeed would be any heart that was not moved by your words on behalf of Samaritan House and the people you serve there. Ed told me that you had fears about your skills as an orator, but in my opinion, you may rest assured on that score. Your words and your tone displayed a rare sensitivity to your audience and your cause. I have every expectation that your efforts will produce positive results.

I regret that I was unable to visit the mission before leaving India Bay, but my children were awaiting my visit here. I marvel that they are so anxious to see me, for I am not the attentive father I should be. But I do love my three young ones, and to share the holidays with them is invigorating. Max, the eldest, is ten years old, and he seems to me to grow by feet between the times I am with him. Lulu—her Christian name is Lucilla, but she prefers her pet name—is a bright and impetuous child of almost nine years, inclined to harmless mischief, I fear, but devoted to her brother and sister. The "baby" is Gracie, who is now five. She is a delicate child, and full of love. At times, she displays wisdom far beyond my own. I wish that I could keep them with me, but my schedule is so erratic, and it is not practical. Their aunt takes good care of them, I'm certain, and it is important—don't you think?—for children of their age to have a mother figure to guide their upbringing. My own life is perhaps too close to that of a confirmed bachelor to be of much benefit to my children.

At this point, Vi stopped reading. *Is it strange that he should write to me of such personal matters?* she asked herself. *Do I deceive myself, or is he seeking advice?* She shook her head in puzzlement and continued reading the professor's letter.

On the subject of children, I hope that the Evans sisters are recovering from their loss. Nothing could be so devastating for children as the death of their mother. Perhaps I will have the opportunity to meet with the girls in the near future. I will be returning to India Bay near the end of January on some academic business. If it is agreeable to you, I should very much like to come to Samaritan House and see the children. But I rely entirely on your opinion. If you think such a visit would give the girls more pain than solace, I defer to your judgment. In any case, it would give me great pleasure to see the work you and your friends are doing at the mission. I shall be staying at the Bayside Hotel, so I can call at any time it is convenient.

Again, please accept my sincere gratitude for your gracious welcome to a stranger. I hope you will remember me to Mrs. O'Flaherty, Miss Clayton, and Dr. Bowman.

Respectfully,
Marcus Darius Raymond

"Well," Vi said aloud as she removed her eyeglasses and sat back in her chair. Contemplating the contents of the letter, Vi was quite unaware of the smile that brightened her face and highlighted her dimple.

"Well, well," she said again.

"Well what?" a voice said, startling Vi so that she dropped the letter, and the pages drifted to the floor.

"I'm sorry, Vi girl," said Mrs. O'Flaherty. "I didn't mean to surprise you. I came to remind you about your meeting this morning."

"You didn't surprise me, Mrs. O," Vi replied as she quickly bent forward to retrieve the fallen letter.

"Actually, you did surprise me," Vi went on in a flustered way that was unusual for her. "But it's all right. I was just reading — I'd just finished reading — I got this letter from Professor Raymond."

Mrs. O'Flaherty asked, "Is he well?"

"I think so," Vi said. "He writes from Boston to thank me for our hospitality. And he says some nice things about my speech at the ball. He asks about Tansy and Marigold, but he doesn't mention everything he did to help them."

"He's being modest," Mrs. O'Flaherty said. "A gentleman does not dwell on his accomplishments."

Vi was shuffling through the pages, putting the letter back in its proper order. "He sends his greetings to you and Emily and Dr. Bowman. Oh, yes, he says he's coming back to India Bay next month and hopes to call on us."

Mrs. O'Flaherty knew her young friend's moods and mannerisms as well as anyone. But she wasn't used to seeing Vi in such a nervous state, and she wondered if the last bit of news from the professor might be the cause.

"Did he say anything else?" the older woman inquired in a casual way.

Vi looked up and said, "He told me about his children. His letter is odd, Mrs. O. It doesn't sound at all like the self-assured man we met. His letter is almost shy — tentative."

Vi held out the pages and said, "You read it, Mrs. O. It's not private. Please read it and tell me what you think."

She stood up and almost shook the pages of the letter at Mrs. O'Flaherty, who took them from her hand.

Vi glanced at her watch and said, "Mr. Fredericks should be here at any minute." She brushed her skirt and patted her hair as she added, "God willing, we may find our schoolteacher today."

Then she exited the office before Mrs. O'Flaherty could say anything else. Vi rushed out so quickly that she failed to notice the amused twinkle in Mrs. O'Flaherty's sapphire eyes.

A half hour later, Vi was in conversation with a nice-looking man just a few years older than she. They were seated in the combined meeting and dining room, where Vi had held so many interviews with potential mission employees.

Vi had already seen several well-qualified candidates, but, alas, each one had expressed reservations about working in Wildwood—the city's poorest and most crime-ridden district. In the end, Vi chose not to accept anyone who approached the task with fear or prejudice. Now, with classes set to start in only three weeks, she was feeling worried, though she found comfort in the words of Philippians 4:6: "Do not be anxious about anything, but in everything, by prayer and petition, with thanksgiving, present your requests to God."

As Vi and the young man chatted, she found herself growing increasingly hopeful. Mr. Fredericks was a graduate of a prestigious Southern university. He had been teaching at the Boys' Academy for a year, and Vi's twin brothers,

Herbert and Harold Travilla, were among his students. The headmaster of the academy and the twins had eagerly recommended Mr. Fredericks to Vi.

Vi asked, "Have you taught young children before? Our pupils will range in age from six to twelve years."

Mr. Fredericks replied, "I haven't taught little children, but I helped my mother instruct my younger brothers before I left home for college. It was something I liked very much."

"There are twenty-four boys and girls who will be coming in January," Vi said, "and they will be quite different from your brothers and the students at the academy."

"All I can say is that I feel sure I can manage," the teacher said.

For some reason, Vi believed that he could. They talked at some length about matters including curriculum and discipline in the classroom, and Mr. Fredericks asked intelligent questions, which pleased Vi. He expressed sincere interest in the Wildwood community and showed no hint of fear or prejudice when Vi spoke of the impoverished circumstances of the area and its residents.

After the interview, Vi conducted Mr. Fredericks on a tour of the mission and introduced him to Mrs. O'Flaherty, Zoe, and the three little girls. Vi paid close attention to the girls' reaction to Mr. Fredericks.

As he prepared to leave, Vi said, "If you are still interested, I would like you to consider the position. We haven't discussed salary, however. Would it be agreeable if I write to you of that?"

"I assume you need my answer quickly," he said.

"I do," she replied. "But I also want you to have sufficient time to evaluate the offer. Our students will present different challenges than those who attend the Boys' Academy. The children of Wildwood know nothing of privilege. Some will suffer from poor health. Others will have little experience of personal discipline. They will not all be Christian or of any faith. You need to consider your choice carefully."

"I will, Miss Travilla," he said with gravity. "But all your students are children, whatever their situation, and education may be the key that unlocks the door of poverty and struggle for them. I would feel fortunate to take part in that process."

Vi smiled and said, "I hope to see you again soon, Mr. Fredericks."

"I am sure that you will, Miss Travilla," he replied, grinning broadly as he took his leave.

Vi immediately reported the details of the interview to Mrs. O'Flaherty, Zoe, and Emily Clayton, the nurse who ran the mission's medical clinic. Vi told them what had been discussed, and the more she said, the more her friends agreed with her decision to offer him the job.

"When will you know his answer?" Zoe asked.

"Soon, I hope," Vi said. "If he says 'yes,' it will be the best of Christmas gifts."

Before bed that night, Vi asked Mrs. O'Flaherty to her room and told her about the letter from Adelaide Allison. With hopeful hearts, they prayed that the next news would bring confirmation that Tansy and Marigold's family had been found at last.

Then Mrs. O'Flaherty mentioned Professor Raymond's letter.

"I don't want to read too much into what he wrote," Vi said.

Violet's Perplexing Puzzles

"Nor do I," Mrs. O'Flaherty agreed. "But I sense that he is troubled. Being with his children for the holidays, he may be questioning his decision not to keep his family together. Still, he's hardly the only widower who has ever been in such a situation."

"That's probably it," Vi said. "He loves his children, and being with them, it would be natural for him to feel some regret about the time they spend apart."

"Since he raised the subject in his letter, he may wish to discuss it further when he visits in January," Mrs. O'Flaherty noted. "Would you be willing to assist him if he does ask for advice?"

"Of course," Vi said firmly. Then she retreated, saying, "I think I would, but what do I know of widowed fathers and their children?"

"Will you reply to his letter?"

"I will. Tomorrow I'll write to extend our invitation to visit the mission," Vi replied a little primly. "A polite response is called for."

"It is," Mrs. O'Flaherty said with a wry little smile.

Then they talked over some of the mission's business, particularly the plans for Christmas, and nothing more was said of the professor and his problems. Vi, however, could not so easily dismiss his letter from her thoughts. His words confused her, and she had no idea what he might need of her. But she did know one way that she could help. From that night forward, Vi made a special point to include Professor Raymond and his three youngsters in her prayers. She knew their names now—Max and Lulu and Gracie—and somehow that made her feel as if she knew them. She asked for the Lord's blessing on the professor and each of the children she had never met.

CHAPTER 2

Holiday Surprises

*Then they opened their treasures
and presented him with gifts of
gold and of incense and
of myrrh.*

<small>MATTHEW 2:11</small>

Holiday Surprises

*O*nly six days remained until Christmas, and Samaritan House was in high gear. It had been decided that the mission would serve a special dinner on the afternoon before Christmas, followed by a brief worship service. Vi asked Mr. Williams—the pastor of Christine and Enoch's church in Boxtown, the section of Wildwood where most of the city's black families lived—to lead the service with Reverend Stephens, the minister to one of Wildwood's white congregations.

Knowing that the black and white people of Wildwood lived separately, Vi was worried that the two men might be afraid to cause dissension between the segregated communities, but both welcomed the opportunity to come together to worship. Reverend Stephens said he would be pleased to stand side by side with his fellow servant of the Lord. Mr. Williams sent a cheerful note accepting Vi's invitation. "A meal tastes better when it is well seasoned," he wrote. "I believe this will be the first meal ever in Wildwood to be seasoned with pepper *and* salt."

There would be presents for every child who came to the mission, and Zoe and Emily took charge of buying the gifts. Vi had hoped to have presents for the adults as well, but there just wasn't time to organize such a bounty. Because more and more people were coming to Samaritan House, there were so many new needs that there was barely enough time in each day to accomplish what was necessary.

Vi did make time to write to Professor Raymond. After she'd mailed the letter, she gave herself a firm little lecture:

Professor Raymond is a grown man and a very smart one. He can handle his problems quite well. Your concerns are right here in Wildwood, not in Boston. You must concentrate on the responsibilities at hand. Mark Raymond can manage his life quite well without your assistance.

During her busy days, she mostly succeeded at pushing aside thoughts of the Raymond family. But at night, when the mission was quiet, she could not keep them away. When she read to Tansy and Marigold and listened to their bedtime prayers, her thoughts inevitably traveled to the three children in Boston. She wondered if Professor Raymond might be at their bedsides and hearing their prayers.

On the Saturday before Christmas, dark clouds rolled in from the sea, and all of India Bay was drenched in a cold and relentless rainstorm. But the downpour did not dampen the holiday mood inside Samaritan House.

Zoe had a special chore for the girls. After breakfast, she took Tansy, Marigold, and Polly to the schoolroom, where the large worktable was heaped with scraps of fabrics, ribbons, and laces. There were stacks of paper, plenty of coloring pencils, jars of paste, and several pairs of scissors.

"We are going to make decorations for the Christmas tree," Zoe said.

The little girls looked one to another. "Miss Vi didn't tell us there would be a tree," Tansy said in a questioning way.

"Miss Vi doesn't know," Zoe said in a happy whisper. "Vi's mother, her brothers and sister, and her grandparents are coming here tomorrow after church, but Vi has no idea of their plans. They are bringing some things for the mission, and they've promised to include a beautiful tree. Mrs. Travilla asked me to buy some decorations, but I had a better idea. I always think that it's nicer to have decorations made with loving hands, but I knew I couldn't make everything myself. I needed help from someone I could depend on. *Who?* I wondered. *Why, it's plain as the nose on your face*, I answered myself. *There's Tansy and Marigold and Polly!* So will you help me?"

The girls were already giggling at Zoe. Now they shouted a chorus of yeses, and hugged Zoe in their excitement.

Zoe put her finger to her lips and said, "We have to be quiet, so Vi doesn't hear us and become curious. She's at work in her office, and Polly's mother has promised to keep her downstairs until lunchtime. So we have all morning to work."

Polly and Marigold decided to make a paper chain to encircle the tree, and they were soon busily cutting and pasting. Zoe showed Tansy how to make little dolls from paper. They wrapped and glued white paper into cone shapes and then drew simple faces on the pointed ends. To finish the dolls, they added dresses of fabric and lace and pasted on little wings cut from silver paper.

"They're like angels," Marigold said when she examined the first two of the finished paper dolls.

"They will remind us of the angels that announced the birth of our Lord to the shepherds in the fields," Zoe said.

"It will be a Christmas story tree!" Tansy said.

Zoe looked thoughtfully at Tansy and said, "What a grand idea. A Christmas story tree filled with ornaments that remind us of God's greatest gift to us—the Lord Jesus. Can you girls think of other things we might make?"

"Stars, Miss Zoe," said Polly immediately, "for the star in the east that the wise men followed."

"Perfect!" Zoe enthused.

Tansy said, "The wise men brought gifts for the baby. But how could we make gold and frankincense and myrrh? I don't even know what frankincense and myrrh are."

"They are fragrant parts of plants used for incense and were very valuable," Zoe said. Her lovely brow wrinkled as she thought how they might create decorations that would symbolize the gifts of the three Magi. She happened to look down at one of the paper cones that lay on the table.

"I know!" she said excitedly. "We can make more of these cones in gold paper. I have some dried lavender, and I'm sure Polly's mother would give us some cloves and cinnamon from the pantry. We can fill the gold cones with lavender and spices to be symbols of the sweet-smelling incense brought by the three kings who traveled so far to see the baby Jesus."

The girls agreed that this was a wonderful idea. But Marigold's face wore a confused look. "What's a symbol?" she asked.

"It's something that stands for something else," Zoe replied. "We see a symbol, and it reminds us of something else."

"Like the cross," Tansy said. "The cross makes us think of Jesus and how He gave His life to save us all. It makes us think about His suffering for our sakes."

Smiling at the older girl, Zoe said, "That's an excellent explanation, Tansy. When we see a cross, we think about how Jesus came to earth as a man and became a teacher and healer. And we remember how He died for our sins and then rose from the dead so that we would know His promise of reunion with Him in Heaven."

"But our paper chain, Miss Zoe?" Polly said in a questioning tone. "The Bible doesn't say anything about paper chains. Is it a symbol?"

"Yes, your beautiful chain is a symbol too," Zoe said. "You've cut strips of colorful paper to make circles. And you've joined the circles together to make the links of your chain. Think about a circle, girls. Where does it begin and where does it end?"

All three girls pondered for several moments. Marigold spoke first. "I don't know where a circle starts, Miss Zoe," she said. "A circle just goes round and round."

"It has no start or ending," Zoe said. "To many people, a circle symbolizes God's never-ending love. In God, there is no beginning or end. You know what Jesus teaches us in John 3:16: 'For God so loved the world that he gave his one and only Son, that whoever believes in him shall not perish but have eternal life.' When we encircle the Christmas tree with your paper chain, it will be a symbol of God's gift of eternal life to everyone who believes in Him."

Marigold and Polly looked at their work with fresh eyes. They saw not just a pretty paper chain, but an expression of God's limitless love.

"We better make it real beautiful," Polly said softly to Marigold.

"I know," Marigold replied in a whisper. "It's a *symbol*, and it's got to be really, really special."

Zoe overheard the girls' remarks, and her heart swelled with love. She went to stand between their chairs, bent down, and put her arms around their shoulders. Hugging them gently, she said, "If you two will continue making this splendid chain, Tansy and I will collect the flowers and spices. Do you mind if we leave you alone for a while?"

"We'll be just fine, Miss Zoe," Marigold said with her brightest smile. "Me and Polly have work to do. Making a symbol is important, isn't it?"

"Very, very important," Zoe said.

At lunch, the girls were very careful to say nothing that might reveal the secret about the Christmas tree. But Mrs. O'Flaherty didn't miss the giggles and mischievous nudges that passed between the children. Since she knew the details of the Travillas and Dinsmores' planned visit, Mrs. O'Flaherty had an idea of the reason for the girls' high spirits.

Vi also noticed their good moods but assumed it was only their anticipation of the holidays. She might have been more attentive if she hadn't been so excited herself.

On this day, Dr. Bowman was in attendance for the residents' lunch, and Vi asked him to say the blessing. When he finished his prayer, Mrs. O'Flaherty began passing bowls of hearty chicken and vegetable soup.

When everyone was served, Vi stood and said, "Before we eat, I have something to tell you. I received a letter this morning, and Mr. Seth Fredericks has agreed to become our teacher. Our school will open on the seventh day of January as we'd all hoped. God has brought us a new gift, so will you all join me in a prayer of thanks?"

Heads were bowed, and Vi began, "Dearest Father in Heaven, You have once again heard our call for help and answered our need. Thank You for sending Mr. Fredericks to Samaritan House. Please look upon him with favor as he teaches the children. Thank You, Lord, for sending us one who will bring knowledge to the children. Strengthen us, Lord, so we may help Mr. Fredericks as he takes on this challenge. And bless him, his students, and all of us as we learn together. Amen."

Vi had been forced to make some difficult decisions about the running of the mission. There was always someone at Samaritan House to open the door to anyone in need. But it was not possible for the small staff to work around the clock. So Vi—after consulting with her family and her friends at the mission—came up with a schedule. The clinic would be open each weekday from nine o'clock in the morning until half past four in the afternoon and until noon on Saturday. The school would meet from half past eight till noon, and the students would have lunch after their classes. The daily meal for the people of Wildwood would be served at four o'clock every afternoon—except Sunday. Sundays were reserved for the residents of the house to worship and rest.

Vi tried to go home to Ion on Sundays whenever she could; otherwise she and Mrs. O'Flaherty attended one of the local churches in Wildwood. The Reeves and Tansy and Marigold had become regular participants in the Sunday services at Mr. Williams's church in Boxtown. Mary and Polly Appleton belonged to a small congregation that met in an old house not far from the mission.

Over the past two months, they had fallen into a comfortable Sunday routine. After church, Mrs. O'Flaherty and Vi prepared lunch—giving Mary a respite from the kitchen—and then everyone shared Bible study and devotion. The adults would go over the mission's needs for the next week, and in the evening, everyone assembled again for Bible reading and prayers. In general, Sunday was a quiet day at Samaritan House, and Vi looked forward to the peacefulness. It was a day for her to contemplate the activities of the week just past, to plan for the week ahead, and to seek God's guidance as she evaluated the former and anticipated the latter.

She fully expected the Sunday before Christmas to be no different, so she was not prepared for the arrival of two carriages and a cart. The residents were just completing their afternoon devotion when there was a banging at the front door. *It must be Ed,* Vi thought, *for no one else insists on hammering at the door when there is a bell. But why has he come today? I hope nothing is wrong at Ion.*

She hurried to the entry hall, not seeing the knowing smiles of her friends or hearing the excited whispers of Marigold and Polly. She opened the door, and there stood Ed—with her mother, the twins, Rosemary, Danny, their grandparents, and Ben and Crystal! Vi's mouth flew open in astonishment as her family shouted out a gleeful "Merry Christmas!"

"We come bearing gifts," Ed said with a grin.

"But you didn't tell me you would visit today," Vi said with a happy laugh.

"You are the only one we didn't tell," said Elsie, giving her daughter a warm hug and a kiss. "This is our surprise for you, and the gifts we bring are for the mission. We decided that would please you more than anything for yourself."

"Oh, it does, Mamma!" Vi said, returning the hug.

The family came in, but Ed, the twins, Danny, and Ben went back outside and began removing items from the vehicles. The mission's entry hall was soon stacked with boxes, bags, and baskets, all filled to their brims.

"What is this bounty?" Vi asked.

"Gifts and necessities, my dear," said Horace Dinsmore, Jr., as he laid his arm around his granddaughter's shoulder.

"Zoe told us that you have presents for children but not adults," Harold said, "so Mamma and Grandmamma have brought grown-up gifts."

Herbert added, "Harry and I helped wrap them."

"There's some boxes of clothes, too," Danny said. "Mamma said that Samaritan House should have a closet of clothing for people who don't have warm things to wear. We've been collecting them from everybody in the whole family."

"Don't forget the blankets," Rose Dinsmore said. "Your Aunt Rosie appealed to her church group, and they have sent two boxes of warm blankets for you to distribute."

"And there's food for your Christmas Eve meal," Rosemary chimed in. "Grandpapa brought two of his best hams, and Crystal has baked pies and breads. See over there," she said, pointing to a large crate. "Those are fresh oranges sent up from Viamede by Cousin Isa and Cousin James."

Vi looked around at all the containers and then at her beloved family. Her eyes welled with tears of gratitude. "How can I ever thank you?" she said. "All of this — I never imagined. Oh, you are the very best family in the world!"

Vi turned to Mrs. O'Flaherty and asked, "Did you know, Mrs. O?"

"I did, and since it was a *good* secret, I was able to keep it to myself," Mrs. O'Flaherty responded. "We all did."

"Even my young friends?" Vi said, looking at the girls.

"Yes, ma'am, we kept the secret too," Tansy replied, while Marigold and Polly giggled behind their hands.

"Well, I will forgive you all for not telling me," Vi laughed merrily, "as long as you will help me find places for these wonderful gifts."

Violet's Perplexing Puzzles

With some confusion and a great deal of laughter, they began to empty the boxes and bags and put everything away. Ben and Crystal helped Mary take the food to the kitchen, while the others removed the remaining items to the storage room off of the entry hall. As the adults sorted through the items, Vi discovered several boxes of toys.

Rosemary quickly organized Danny, Tansy, Marigold, and Polly. Their arms loaded with toys, they marched up the stairs to a little room that had been set aside as a place for youngsters whose parents were visiting the clinic. Zoe managed to whisper something to Tansy, and the girl gave a knowing smile in reply.

Vi made another discovery—a large box of books.

At her side, Zoe said in a low voice, "Those are from Ed and your grandfather. They know you have the schoolbooks you need, so they went through their shelves for works of fiction. I knew Ed had a taste for adventure books, but I hadn't thought that Uncle Horace was also an adventure reader. Aunt Rose and I helped him pack these books a couple of weeks ago. He was very careful to select appropriate reading, but he was like a boy himself as he told us when he had first read this book and that one."

"Grandpapa can seem severe at times," Vi said, "but he has the kindest heart, doesn't he?"

"I remember being a little afraid of him when we all first met in Rome," Zoe said. "I thought him very strict, compared to my darling Papa. Now, I thank our Lord every day for putting me in the care of your grandparents when Papa died. They are the most loving and generous people. And do you know? I like Uncle Horace's strictness, for I understand now that he is teaching me self-discipline. I had precious little of that when I arrived at The Oaks two years ago," she said with a charming laugh.

"What are you two gossiping about?" came Ed's chipper voice from behind them.

"Not gossip," Zoe said. "Vi and I were discussing Uncle Horace's and your taste for adventure novels."

Ed bent to pick up the heavy box. "I'll take this to the schoolroom," he said as he headed to the stairs. "I still think you were gossiping, for I doubt that old adventure books would bring on such girlish giggles."

"Your brother inherited much of Uncle Horace's strictness," Zoe said when Ed was out of earshot. " 'Girlish giggles' indeed! You'd think we were a pair of teenagers at our first cotillion."

"But you are a teenager," Vi chuckled, "and I'm barely six months away from it. Ed was just teasing."

"Well, I wish he would tease someone else," Zoe replied with a flash of temper that surprised Vi. "He can be so infuriating! I don't like being treated as a child. Not at all."

***

The unpacking completed, the adults gathered in the meeting room, and Christine and Crystal brought in two trays of steaming cups. The aroma of apples and cinnamon filled the air.

"Thought you folks would enjoy some hot apple cider," Crystal said.

Vi jumped up from her seat and said, "Please join us, Crystal. Christine and I will pass the cups if you will get Ben and Enoch and Mary."

Vi began handing out the cups of cider with a warning: "Don't drink yet. I think we should have a toast."

Crystal returned with Ben and Mary. She said, "Enoch's doing something. He wants you to go on without him."

Violet's Perplexing Puzzles

"Yes, let's go ahead," Harold said. "The cider will cool if we wait."

When everyone was served, Vi asked her grandfather to make the toast. Horace's words were full of good cheer, but as she listened, Vi suddenly realized that Ed was not in the room. *He must be upstairs with the children*, she thought with a little disappointment.

Horace ended his toast with a jovial command that everyone lift their cups "to Samaritan House and to all who find help, hope, and the spirit of our loving Savior within its walls."

Cups were clinked, and everyone was sipping the deliciously warm fruit juice when suddenly, the front door flew open with a loud bang. A gust of cold wind blew in.

They all turned toward the entry hall, where a beaming Ed and a grinning Enoch were coming through the door carrying a thick evergreen tree. Holding the trunk end was Dr. Bowman. (Having been alerted to the secret, he could not miss the surprise.) The twins rushed to help and within a couple of minutes, the tall tree stood beside the foot of the stairs in the entry. The children had lined up on the stairs. Rosemary was holding baby Jacob, who was clapping and squealing with delight.

"It's beautiful!" Vi exclaimed. "But we have no decorations."

"Yes, we do, Miss Vi!" Marigold called out. She was hopping up and down with excitement. "We made them for you!"

Danny and Tansy held up two baskets full of shining and colorful items.

"You've thought of everything," Vi said. "Absolutely everything!"

"It's time to decorate," Ed proclaimed. "Tansy tells me that this is a Christmas story tree. Each ornament is a symbol of our Lord Jesus' birth and His gift of salvation. I understand we are to begin with a chain of paper—each circle representing God's unending love. Do you have the chain, girls?"

Marigold and Polly lifted up part of what was many yards of bright paper.

"Then let's get to work," Ed said.

With all the young people helping, the paper chain was draped from top to bottom. The handmade angels, stars, animals cut from paper and colored with pencils, and golden cones soon hung from every bough. Zoe had cut delicate paper snowflakes as a symbol of the Christmas season, and these added to the overall magic of the tree.

The merriment continued for several hours, so it was dark when the family and Dr. Bowman departed. Enoch quickly locked up for the night while Zoe and Mrs. O'Flaherty helped Mary ready the utensils and ingredients for the next day's meal—their special Christmas Eve dinner.

After hearing the prayers of two very sleepy girls, Vi tucked Tansy and Marigold in their bed. Then she joined the adults in the kitchen.

"I wonder how many will come tomorrow," Zoe said.

"We never know," Vi replied. "It could be a handful or it could be several dozen."

"We've got more than enough for three or four dozen," Mary said. "I'm thinking we'll have a crowd. Word's gone round about dinner at the mission at four o'clock. Folks know they can count on a good meal, but I expect our Christmas tree is going to make their eyes pop!"

CHAPTER

3

Days of Celebration

*But when you give a banquet,
invite the poor, the crippled,
the lame, the blind, and
you will be blessed.*

LUKE 14:13–14

*M*ary guessed right. The people who came to the clinic on Christmas Eve morning were all surprised by the beautiful Christmas tree in the entry hall of Samaritan House.

"Ain't that tree a pretty sight," said Mr. Calisher, the blacksmith, who stopped in to have Miss Clayton look at a painful boil on his neck.

"All them stars and little angels...why, it almost takes my breath away," agreed old Widow Amos, who'd come for a refill of cough elixir.

"I haven't seen a tree like that since I did housekeeping for that rich family on the other side of town," said Miss Bessie Moran, who ran a boardinghouse two streets south of the mission.

They had another surprise when they entered the clinic, for Dr. Bowman was there along with Miss Clayton.

"Thought you only came on Fridays, Doc," observed Mr. Calisher.

"I didn't want to miss that delicious meal the ladies are serving this afternoon," Dr. Bowman replied as he led the blacksmith to a little cubicle off the main clinic area.

Downstairs in the kitchen, the ladies were "cooking up a storm," as Christine said. The usual afternoon meal was hearty but simple (Mary Appleton's chicken and dumplings was a favorite). For their Christmas Eve meal, however, the menu was a feast—ham, roasted chicken, sweet potatoes, onions baked in cream, green beans, cornbread, pecan and apple pie, and a fresh Viamede orange for everyone. With the food brought from Ion and The Oaks, there was little fear of running short. In fact, Vi and Christine had already packed a number of food baskets, which Enoch and Dr. Bowman would deliver to some of their ill and elderly neighbors.

Almost fifty people came to the mission's table that afternoon. All ages were represented, from tiny babies to the very elderly. Vi had met most of the guests before, at the mission or on the streets of Wildwood. But there were new faces too, and Vi welcomed these strangers as friends — ushering them to seats at the long, plain wood tables, which almost filled the large meeting and dining room.

At the stroke of four, the kitchen door swung open, and Christine entered, carrying a large tray of filled plates. She was followed by Mrs. O'Flaherty, Emily, and Mary Appleton, each bearing a similar tray, and the food was quickly distributed.

Vi said a blessing over the food, and the guests began to eat. There would be time for greetings and prayers afterwards. Vi had learned that hunger brought people to the mission's meals — the kind of deep and gnawing hunger that pushed everything else from a person's mind. Christmas Eve was no different from any other day for people who, until the opening of the mission, rarely saw a full plate or experienced the satisfaction of a full stomach.

There was very little talking at first, but as the meal progressed (with second helpings for all who wanted more), the mood changed. The house was warm and so was the companionship. People who offered little more than a nod to each other when they passed on the streets of Wildwood found themselves in conversations. And the mission ladies took time, when they weren't serving food, to sit a while and talk and listen.

Reverend Stephens and his wife had arrived early to help, and Mr. Williams came at five o'clock, when Vi and the others were passing out plates of pie to the guests. Now, it must be admitted that most of the people wondered at the appearance of a well-dressed black man in their midst, and there was a good deal of whispering that he might be a new servant at the mission. But their questions were answered when Vi addressed the gathering.

"I want to thank all of you for sharing our first Christmas at Samaritan House," she said. "It means the world to us that you join our celebration of the birth of our Lord Jesus. I've invited two friends of the mission — Reverend Stephens and Mr. Williams — to lead us in a brief service of prayer and thanksgiving. I hope all of you will stay, but if you must leave, please accept my gratitude that you were able to join us on this very special day."

Vi expected to see people getting up, for she knew that the presence of a black minister would shock many of the white residents of Wildwood. Zoe and Emily had gone to the entry hall to help with coats and hand out gifts to those who chose to leave. But to Vi's surprise, no one stood. All eyes remained on her, and after a minute, she said with a wide smile, "I guess we're ready to begin. Reverend Stephens, will you lead us in prayer?"

The minister stepped forward. After a few words expressing his pleasure at being included in Samaritan House's first Christmas, he offered a prayer of thanks to God for His greatest gift — the birth of a poor child in Bethlehem whose short life brought the promise of salvation to all humankind. When he finished, Mr. Williams came to stand at his side. Opening his Bible, he read the Christmas story from the first and second chapters of Matthew: " 'This is how the birth of Jesus came about....' "

Then Reverend Stephens spoke about the earthly life of Jesus—a life of service that provides the model for every man, woman, and child. Mr. Williams concluded with a prayer thanking the Lord for His love that never fails.

From the back of the room rose a strong and clear voice. "O little town of Bethlehem, how still we see thee lie," Mrs. O'Flaherty sang. On the next line, she was joined by the children: "Above thy deep and dreamless sleep, the silent stars go by." The mission ladies and the pastors added their voices—"Yet in thy dark streets shineth the everlasting Light"—and Vi gestured for everyone to sing. Some did, and though their voices were not trained and in some cases not on key, they sang with glad hearts. "The hopes and fears of all the years are met in thee tonight."

The meeting room echoed with joyful song as they completed the hymn. Mrs. O'Flaherty started another—"Hark! The Herald Angels Sing"—and even the shyest of the guests added their voices.

Night closed in on Wildwood Street, and though they wanted to linger, people began to leave. Each person received a wrapped gift as they departed—warm scarves or gloves or socks for everyone. The children also received brightly wrapped packages that contained small toys and some sweet candies.

Vi stood at the door to bid good night to all.

"You done something mighty good for us, miss," said Widow Amos, a woman well past seventy years who was accompanied by her grandson, a tall boy whom Vi had seen working at the livery stable.

"I hope you enjoyed the meal, Mrs. Amos," Vi said.

"Why, sure we did," the woman replied, "but I was speaking 'bout bringing us together here tonight. You may not know it, but there was people here who ain't been outta their houses or spoke to their neighbors in years. Folks so broken by being poor that they've just about given up on living. But here they were, sharing your food and talking and some of 'em singing 'bout the little babe born in the stable. It was a wonder to behold, miss. Just a wonder."

"Thank you for telling me that, Mrs. Amos," Vi said gratefully.

The elderly woman put her hand on Vi's arm and said, "You keep it up. This ain't easy work, and there's still folks who don't want you here in Wildwood. But you be strong and trust the good Lord."

"I will," Vi said. "Samaritan House is part of Wildwood now, and we intend to stay."

The widow looked into Vi's eyes and smiled. "I believe you will," she said firmly. "Yes, indeedee, I believe you will."

When the last of the visitors had departed, Vi and the others talked about their first Christmas Eve gathering as they cleaned up. They all had stories to tell about the people they'd met and the conversations they'd had. The Widow Amos wasn't the only one who felt that something special had been achieved that night.

Mr. Williams and Reverend and Mrs. Stephens had left soon after the last of the guests, but not before thanking Vi and the others for including them in the activities. Mrs. Stephens had renewed her offer to assist at the mission, and she and Vi made plans to host a tea for the wives of the other pastors in Wildwood in the week after New Year's Day.

Before Emily and Dr. Bowman departed, they both expressed their intention to come to Samaritan House the next day. Doctor Bowman told Vi, "Since the Reeves are going to Ion with you ladies, Mary and young Polly will be alone. There's a good chance people will come by the mission, and Mary will need help. Miss Clayton and I have both arranged to have our Christmas lunches early, so we can be here until your return."

Vi had protested, but Emily and Dr. Bowman would not bend, and at last Vi gave in. It was a good thing, too, since a goodly number of people did come to the mission the next day, and Mary found herself serving a full meal to those who had no homes to go to on Christmas Day.

Christmas morning was cold and clear, and the residents who were going to Ion dressed in their warmest clothing. They were cramped inside the closed carriage, but no one minded. Christine held baby Jacob; Tansy and Marigold settled onto Vi's and Mrs. O'Flaherty's laps; and Zoe's pretty face could barely be seen above the packages she held. Only Enoch, in the driver's seat, was unburdened.

The streets of India Bay were nearly deserted—an unusual sight in the busy city—and once they reached the county road, it was also free of the normal traffic.

"It's too quiet!" Zoe declared. "I think we should sing!"

"Good idea," agreed Mrs. O'Flaherty, "for this is the day that all Christians celebrate with songs of thanksgiving. Do you girls know 'Joy to the World'?"

In answer, Marigold broke into song. She was instantly joined by the others, except little Jacob, who clapped and bounced on his mother's knee.

Days of Celebration

When they finished, Vi suggested one of her favorites, "God Rest You Merry Gentlemen," and everyone raised their voices in the traditional "tidings of comfort and joy." Then Zoe asked Mrs. O'Flaherty if there were Irish songs they might learn.

"I can teach you one that might take us all the way to Ion," Mrs. O'Flaherty said. "Some say it came from Ireland. It's called 'The Twelve Days of Christmas.' Each line is about a gift given on one of the twelve days before Christmas. It seems simple, but there's a trick to the singing. Every line is longer than the last one because you must add the gifts together until you have sung all twelve verses. If you forget an item, you have to go back to the beginning and start again."

"It's like a game!" Tansy cried.

"It is," Mrs. O'Flaherty agreed. "It was used to teach Catholic children about their faith in the days when their religion was banned in Ireland. It begins like this—'On the first day of Christmas, my true love gave to me, a partridge in a pear tree.' Now you sing it."

"That's easy, Mrs. O," Marigold said.

Mrs. O'Flaherty smiled and said, "It gets harder. The next verse is this."

She again lifted her voice and sang in her rich contralto, " 'On the second day of Christmas, my true love gave to me, two turtle doves and a partridge in a pear tree.' "

"Oh, I understand," Tansy said. "Will you tell us all the twelve gifts, Mrs. O?"

"Certainly," Mrs. O'Flaherty smiled. "There's a partridge in a pear tree, then two turtle doves, three French hens, four calling birds, five golden rings, six geese a'laying, seven swans a'swimming, eight maids a'milking, nine ladies dancing, ten lords a'leaping, eleven pipers piping, and twelve drummers drumming.

"Each gift is a symbol of faith," Mrs. O'Flaherty went on. "The partridge in a pear tree is Jesus Christ the Son of God. God Himself is the "true love" who gives the good gifts. The two turtle doves stand for the Old and New Testaments and the three French hens symbolize faith, hope, and charity."

"It's like our Christmas tree at the mission!" Tansy said. "All our decorations are symbols, and symbols help us to learn something important. Oh, please, Mrs. O, teach us the whole song."

Mrs. O'Flaherty shared the hidden meaning of the rest of the gifts, and then the singing began. As she predicted, many mistakes were made, and the singers often started over, but that was the fun. When they at last got through all twelve verses without a single error, Mrs. O'Flaherty taught them a variation that was harder; as they sang, each person had to add a line when she pointed to them. This brought much confusion and a great deal of laughter. They had just completed a perfect round when Enoch called down, "Ion ahead!"

Vi looked from the carriage window and saw her home. Her grandfather, her Uncle Trip Dinsmore, and Ed were just coming out of the front door, and they began waving as the carriage pulled beneath the portico. The gentlemen helped the ladies and the children down, and Ed courteously relieved Zoe of the Christmas packages she was holding.

Soon they were all gathered in the parlor with the rest of the family. Vi was seated beside her mother on a sofa, and she slipped her hand over Elsie's. "How good it feels to be at home, Mamma," she said softly.

Elsie clasped her hand and said, "No better than to have you here, my darling daughter."

"What have you planned for us today?" Vi asked.

"Well, the family will dine soon, for I want the servants to have the afternoon for their celebration. Crystal and Aunt Chloe have organized a mid-afternoon meal in the schoolhouse. The women have been cooking for days, and it will be a true feast."

Elsie looked away, casting her glance about the room. Spotting her objective, she asked Marigold and Tansy to come to her. The girls, who had been talking with Rosemary and Danny, hurried to Elsie. She and Vi made a place on the sofa for the girls to sit between them.

"I'm so glad you could be here today," Elsie began. "And so are several other people. Do you remember Aunt Chloe and Miss Crystal?"

"Yes, ma'am, we do," Tansy said happily. "They are the ladies who were very nice to us the first time we visited you. And we saw Miss Crystal just the other day at Samaritan House."

"Well, they have asked a favor of you," Elsie said with a smile. "They want the other people who work here to meet you, so they hope you will join them today. Aunt Chloe and Miss Crystal have planned a big party in the schoolhouse, and they would like you to be their guests. There will be lots of children to meet. Mr. and Mrs. Reeve and Jacob will be going too. Would you enjoy spending the day with them?"

"Yes, Miss Elsie," Marigold said instantly.

"Yes, ma'am, we would," Tansy agreed with a shy smile. "It would be very nice to meet other children."

"That's good," Elsie said. "Now, I have another request."

At the girls' questioning looks, she continued, "I'd like you to keep an eye on Aunt Chloe for me. She is my dearest friend in the world, and I don't want her to tire herself by doing too much today. I want you girls to have fun, but I thought you might check on Aunt Chloe now and then. If she seems weary, you can tell Crystal or Christine."

"We can do that, Mrs. Travilla," Tansy said earnestly. "Aunt Chloe is such a kind lady. She makes me think of my Granny."

Elsie leaned over and kissed both girls on their cheeks. "Thank you, dears," she said. "Now remember, I want you to have a good time and meet lots of people. Just check with Aunt Chloe every once in a while."

"Are you coming to the party, Miss Elsie?" Marigold asked.

"Later in the afternoon," Elsie said. "The children are planning a carol sing, and we wouldn't miss that. Then you'll come back here with us, and we will all exchange our gifts."

Elsie stood, and the girls rose as well. Elsie took their hands and said, "If you'll excuse us, Vi dear, Crystal is waiting for our two young friends."

When Elsie had left with the girls, Vi's grandmother, Rose, and her Aunt Eloise, who was Trip's wife, came to take her place on the sofa. "It is so good to see you, darling," Rose said. "Now tell us all about your first Christmas Eve at Samaritan House."

⁓

The family was summoned to the dining room some twenty minutes later, and after Horace delivered his Christmas blessing, they were served a bountiful meal. But for Vi, there was something far more delicious than the turkey and vegetables and the flaming plum pudding and baked custard that concluded their banquet. It was being once again in the heart of her family.

Looking round at the faces that were all so dear to her and warmed by the companionship of family and friends, she had a thought about how her life had changed: *Yesterday, I was serving dinner at Samaritan House. Today, I am being served in my own home. And my sense of both privilege and gratitude is the same, for each table is the Lord's table. It is His love that surrounds me wherever I am and whoever I am with. Even were I alone today in some distant place, I would not be alone, for He would be with me to warm my solitude. I can never be alone with Him in my heart.*

Her thought carried her forward to a new realization, and her pulse quickened. *I've always known that,* she said to herself, *but here today, among the people I love without reservation—who love You without reservation—I seem to understand more clearly than ever how precious is the family of God. My family at Ion and those at Samaritan House who love You—we are all a part of Your great family. How strange and wonderful this is—to know something without doubt and then, at an unexpected moment, to actually feel it in the deepest part of my heart and soul! Oh, thank You, Father, for giving me this moment and enabling me to put together what is in my mind and in my heart. The meaning of family—of Your great family and Your all-encompassing love for us—it is so real and so clear to me now..."*

A sharp little pain in her arm broke into her prayer. She turned to her right and saw Rosemary's curious face.

"Where were you, Vi?" Rosemary asked with some concern. "Your eyes were closed like you were asleep. Were you daydreaming?"

"Not really," Vi said with a smile so full of gentleness that it surprised Rosemary.

"I was caught up in a thought," Vi added. She would have explained if she could have, but she couldn't capture in words the feeling of God's embrace.

"I'm sorry I pinched you," her sister said, lowering her eyes. "I just did that because I thought you might be asleep. I know how hard you're working at the mission, and I thought maybe you just fell asleep, like I sometimes do when I'm studying."

Vi's smile widened and became her usual bright expression again.

"I wasn't dozing off," she said. "In fact, I've never felt so wide awake. And I forgive you for pinching me. But don't do it again," she added playfully.

"It must have been an important thought," Rosemary said as she took up another forkful of her plum pudding.

"It was," Vi said, "and someday, I'll share it with you."

As Vi returned to her dessert, she happened to overhear Ed speaking to the twins. "Yes, Mark will be back in January," he was saying. "Near the end of the month, he wrote. He'll stay in the city, but you'll have plenty of chances to see him."

"That's great news!" Harold said.

It is great news, Vi thought. The image of Professor Raymond came into her mind — as it so often did these days. She imagined him at his Christmas table, surrounded by his three children, and the picture brought a smile to her lips.

At her side, Rosemary chirped, "Another important thought, Vi?"

"Umm?" Vi replied a little dreamily. "Important? Ah, yes — maybe — oh, I don't know."

Seeing her little sister's curious stare, Vi quickly tried to cover her own confusion.

"Would you like my custard?" Vi asked. "I'm too full to eat it."

The ploy worked, for one of the few things that could distract Rosemary's attention was the offer of a treat.

To distract her own mind, Vi turned to her Uncle Trip and asked him about a recent visit that he and his wife, Eloise, had enjoyed with family members in Chicago, Illinois and in Lansdale, Ohio. Amid talk of their distant relatives, Vi almost succeeded in putting the image of Mark Raymond and his family out of her mind. Almost, but not quite.

CHAPTER

Changes
at the Mission

*God sets the lonely
in families....*

PSALM 68:6

Changes at the Mission

As often happens in the South, the weather made a sudden change to near spring-like temperatures. The warm spell began the day after Christmas, and this in turn brought on an outbreak of colds, coughs, and fevers among the people of Wildwood, which doubled Emily's work in the clinic. Even Mrs. O'Flaherty—who had never been ill to Vi's recollection—came down with a nasty cold and spent several days in bed.

Dr. Bowman came in every day, and given the number of people who appeared at the clinic, his attendance was greatly appreciated. Then Mrs. Stephens stopped by to see Vi on the Monday before New Year's Day. Vi assumed that Mrs. Stephens wanted to discuss the tea party they planned for the wives of the neighborhood ministers, but the lady had something different in mind.

"So many people are sick," Mrs. Stephens began in a tone of urgency, "and cannot care for themselves. Whenever this happens, some of the ladies in our congregation take food to our members who are ill. But there are others in the community who need attention, and I have an idea, Miss Travilla, that we might join forces. We can help in your kitchen and then deliver food to everyone who needs nourishment. Not just our church members, but also those who don't have a church and lack the resources to help themselves."

Vi was immediately taken by Mrs. Stephens's idea. Together with Dr. Bowman and Mary Appleton, they decided how it could be done. Mary said that she could easily increase the amount of food she prepared, and Mrs.

Stephens volunteered herself and the dependable women of her church to assist with the cooking. Dr. Bowman thought that he and Enoch could handle the deliveries, and that would enable the doctor to learn who required medical treatment. Mrs. Stephens said that her husband would accompany them, for he knew the people of Wildwood and who was most in need.

Vi had hoped to begin a home visiting service, but she had not anticipated starting it so soon. Yet the opportunity had presented itself, and she and the others of Samaritan House threw themselves into the project with all their energy. It began that very day, and by the time the outbreak of colds began to subside, the small band of volunteers had become very efficient. Dr. Bowman discovered a great deal about the health problems of many people who could not leave their homes, and they all acquired a much better understanding of the real needs of Wildwood's population.

Mrs. Stephens proved to be a capable organizer, and she persuaded the wives of the pastors of the other Wildwood churches to give their time to the project. Instead of a polite ladies' tea, Vi's first meeting with some of these good ladies was over steaming kettles of soup in the Samaritan House kitchen.

The weather turned chill again after a week, and although this brought other problems, the minor epidemic of colds and fevers soon began to subside. The people who had been ill regained their strength, and most were able to care for themselves again. But the effort had produced a list of people whose needs were continuing — elderly and infirm people who could not come to the mission or attend the churches; families without any income because the head of the house had been injured and could not work; widowed mothers who struggled vainly to keep their children fed and clothed; and people who had no homes. Even though Reverend and Mrs. Stephens had ministered in Wildwood for almost ten years, they were astonished to discover pockets of poverty so desperate that they did not know how people survived.

As the result of what they all learned, it was decided to continue the visiting service. Samaritan House would provide food, and the churches would manage the deliveries. Vi was amazed at how quickly everything had happened. In just two weeks, they had established a program of service that had been a distant goal.

While all this was happening, Vi was also preparing for the opening of the mission school. Seth Fredericks paid several visits to Samaritan House to discuss his duties with Vi. Since many of the students had never attended school before, Mr. Fredericks decided to start them with some simple reading and writing lessons. This way he could evaluate each child's skills and sort them into appropriate levels. He explained his plan to Vi during a meeting in her office. They were going over a list of the students' names and ages, which Vi had prepared.

"But I don't see young Tansy and Marigold here," he said as he studied the list.

"I've decided to let them carry on their lessons with Mrs. O'Flaherty," Vi replied. "Unlike the other youngsters, they have been well taught, and it seems best to continue their individual instruction."

Violet's Perplexing Puzzles

"That is sensible," Mr. Fredericks agreed, adding, "I thought your decision might be because they are Negro."

Vi sat back in her swivel chair and sighed. A pained expression clouded her face. "That was also a consideration," she said. "I had not thought about it until Christine spoke to me. She made me take a hard look at the reality of the girls' situation. Racial prejudices are deeply ingrained, and it could be very difficult for Tansy and Marigold to be the only black children in your class.

"How I hate this divide between the races," she went on, not bothering to hide her anger, "but I cannot expect those two dear children to bear the brunt of it."

"No, you can't," Mr. Fredericks said with a sad shake of his head. "I shall miss having such bright students, but I support your decision—for the girls' sakes."

It had not been an easy choice for Vi. She had only been convinced after several long talks with Christine.

"You've got to face up to the facts, Miss Violet," Christine had told her at last. "If you put Tansy and Marigold in a classroom with white children, there's gonna be trouble. The white children might not be bothered at first, but they're gonna hear things from their parents 'bout how black and white don't mix. And the children are gonna bring those ideas into the school and take 'em out on the girls. That's gonna hurt all the children—black and white. The white children might even leave the school when their parents hear about Tansy and Marigold. If they do keep coming, how they gonna learn when they're all tied up with resentment?"

"But we'll teach them to understand one another," Vi had protested.

"Yes, you will, but it's not a lesson learned quickly. I don't expect I'll live long enough to see the day when black

folks and white folks learn to get along and live like equals. It's sad but true, and we've got to do the best we can with the way things are," Christine said firmly.

"I'm speaking plainly to you, Miss Violet," she continued. "It's not fair to subject those two young girls to bullying and teasing and who knows what else just to teach a lesson to the others. You gotta think about Tansy and Marigold. Right now, those two children are ready to love just about anyone, but how are their feelings gonna change if they run into the kind of prejudice they're likely to experience?"

Vi had known that Christine was right. She didn't like to admit it, but she had to be realistic. Vi longed for the day when the black people of Boxtown would feel comfortable coming to the mission. But even more important was her commitment to Tansy and Marigold. So she'd decided to let them continue their studies with Mrs. O'Flaherty—as would Polly, at the girls' request and with Mary Appleton's approval. It was not the solution that Vi wanted, but after many hours of prayer, she understood that what she wanted was not important when the welfare of the children was at stake.

The school opened in the second week of January as scheduled, and Mr. Fredericks quickly established himself in the esteem of his young pupils. The house was livelier than ever as the children arrived each morning just before nine o'clock and trooped up the stairs to the classroom.

The outbreak of illnesses, the opening of the school, the home visiting service—all these new demands on the mission had occurred in a matter of a few short but exhausting weeks. Vi and the others were literally working from dawn to dusk, and they had hardly a moment to pause and reflect on what was happening. But each night without fail, Vi talked with the Lord and shared with Him all that was in her heart. She told Him of each accomplishment—the small things as well as the big—and sought His help with the problems. Always she thanked Him for leading her to this place and for guiding so many people to their door. And she never forgot to ask His blessing on those closest to her heart—her family and her friends, both near and far.

About a week after the school opened, Vi made an unannounced visit to Ion. Ben's face registered his surprise when he opened the door to her. She greeted him warmly and asked if her mother and brother were in.

"They just went to the library," he said, "and I know they'll be mighty pleased you're here, Miss Violet."

Elsie and Ed were as surprised to see her as Ben had been, and Elsie immediately asked if there was a problem at Samaritan House.

"No, Mamma," Vi assured her as they hugged. "But something has occurred that requires your and Ed's advice without delay. I've received a letter from Aunt Adelaide, and she and Uncle Edward have found the Evans family."

Vi went to the fireplace and began to warm her hands at the cheerfully crackling fire.

"That is grand news," Elsie declared.

"But why so urgent a call?" Ed asked. "It's always good to see you, little sister, but this is very early for you to make the long drive from the city."

As he was speaking, Vi removed a letter and her eyeglasses from her purse. She said, "We now know that Tansy and Marigold have family, and we know where they are. But it raises questions that I don't feel competent to answer on my own. Let me read you Aunt Adelaide's letter."

Dearest Vi,

Our search has ended happily. Our investigator located young Tansy and Marigold's grandparents, and your uncle and I have paid them a visit. They live with their daughter in a village to the north — not far from the border between Pennsylvania and New York. The grandparents, whose names are Oscar and Ethel Evans, are kind and loving people, as is their daughter, a widow whose name is Mrs. Idanell Granger. Our visit proved to be a source of great joy to them, for they have been deeply worried about the whereabouts of the children. They had written to South Carolina after the children did not arrive last summer, but received no reply. Mr. and Mrs. Evans are quite elderly and Mrs. Granger is not strong, so it is not possible for them to travel. They are not well off, though certainly not impoverished. They own their small house, and Mrs. Evans and Mrs. Granger earn income from their sewing. (The grand-mother does only plain sewing now, but Mrs. Granger is a highly skilled embroiderer who does piece work for several ladies' clothiers in Philadelphia.)

Our investigator met them just before New Year's, but Edward and I felt it was our responsibility to inform them of the death of the girls' mother. They were saddened but not surprised, for she had written to them about the true nature and seriousness of her illness. I cannot tell you how thrilled they were to hear that Tansy and Marigold are safe and well cared for.

Violet's Perplexing Puzzles

I won't go into all the details of our visit, because there are more important issues that must be resolved. As I said, the Evanses are elderly, and Mr. Evans is often confined to his bed and requires a great deal of nursing. Mrs. Granger, whom I believe to be nearly sixty, is a sweet and generous person, but frail. I do not think they are capable of raising two energetic young girls. We told them about the children's inheritance, and there was not the slightest hint that the family was interested in the money for themselves. In fact, Mrs. Granger spoke to me privately and expressed her concern that the girls could not receive the education they deserve in the family's community. I asked if the family might be interested in moving to Philadelphia, but she felt such a shift would be too difficult for her parents. And I must agree.

The family is more than willing to take the children in, but Edward and I sensed that they are worried that this may not be the best solution. We left them with the promise that we would contact you and see what other options might be considered. I can assure you that they want to see the girls and will do whatever is in Tansy and Marigold's best interest.

I know you want to discuss this with your mother. Please tell Elsie that my next letter will be to her. And believe me, Vi, your uncle and I are ready to assist you and the children in every way.

Vi finished reading and said that another letter—from Mrs. Granger to the girls—had been included.

"Have you told the children of this?" Elsie asked.

"Not yet," Vi said. "Aunt Adelaide's letter came only yesterday, and I didn't read it until last night. I decided I should talk to you both first. The news is wonderful, but it doesn't solve the question of their future, does it?"

Ed had listened carefully to Adelaide's letter, and he asked Vi if he might read it again. Elsie decided to call for tea, and she left the library to go to the kitchen.

After several minutes, Ed handed the letter back to Vi, and he began slowly pacing the rug in front of the fireplace.

"What are you thinking, brother?" Vi asked.

"That there are a number of possibilities," he replied. "But I think Tansy and Marigold should see their grandparents and aunt as soon as a trip can be arranged. Those kids have been through so much. It seems to me that knowing they have family who love them is just about the most important thing we can do for them right now."

"I agree," Elsie said, returning to the room in time to hear Ed's observation. Vi saw that her mother was smiling.

"I just spoke to Ben and Crystal," Elsie went on, "and asked if they would make a trip to Pennsylvania. I told them what we've learned, and they are both eager to help. Crystal is so fond of the girls, as is Ben. We can organize a trip very soon."

"Oh, Mamma, that's brilliant!" Vi exclaimed.

"It is a beginning," Elsie said. "But I trust Adelaide and Edward's judgment that it may not be feasible for the children to live with their family."

"They could remain at the mission," Ed said. "They are really happy with you there, Vi."

Vi's face fell and she said, "And we all love them so much. But I've been talking with Christine, and I am not sure that the mission is the best place for Tansy and Marigold. Christine is concerned that in Wildwood, the children will be subjected to prejudice and rejection that cannot be avoided. Christine and Enoch have opened my eyes to the terrible truth of racial prejudice. I've seen it—how the children who come to the school stare at the girls, and some even seem fearful of them. I don't think the girls have noticed, but I see it. You understand, Mamma. That's why you want Ben and Crystal to escort the girls to visit their family, isn't it?"

Elsie sat down in the chair next to Vi's and said gently, "I would take them myself, but I know what that would mean. At best, a white woman with two Negro children would be the object of ignorant remarks. I have seen how cruel strangers can be. Much as I would like to meet the Evans family, Ben and Crystal will be much better escorts."

"Then the girls could live here," Ed declared. "Why not? Crystal would adopt them tomorrow. We have plenty of room. Education is no problem, is it, Mamma? The girls could go to the school here and have lots of friends."

"That is an idea," Elsie said thoughtfully. "I would love to have them. But there are many issues to consider, and the most important will be what Tansy and Marigold want. There are people we need to consult before we make any decisions. I want to talk with your grandfather, and I should contact Mr. Bartleby in South Carolina, for there are legal matters of permanent guardianship involved. We cannot rush into a decision that will affect the girls' entire lives."

"But that won't interfere with their trip to Pennsylvania?" Vi questioned.

"Not at all," Elsie said. "There is one piece of advice I have for you, Vi. When you tell the children, offer the trip as their choice. Whatever the problems they have in Wildwood, they have found security at Samaritan House.

You are their family, and they should know that you always will be. They are sensitive children, especially Tansy. They'll need assurance that you will never abandon them, no matter where they go."

Vi smiled and said, "I can do that, Mamma, because it's true. Wherever our little girls are, they will always be in my heart. From them, I've learned how you must feel about us. I mean, how a mother feels about her children."

Elsie leaned toward Vi and took her hand. "It is a feeling that never fades, even when her children are adults."

There was a light tapping at the door, and a servant entered with the tea tray. Vi was soon enjoying a cup of the sweetened brew, though she did not need it to warm herself. The love of her family had already done that.

CHAPTER

5

Departures and Arrivals

Do not plot harm against your neighbor, who lives trustfully near you.

PROVERBS 3:29

*T*ansy and Marigold were overjoyed to learn that their grandparents and aunt had been found. Vi told them as soon as she returned to the mission, and the girls read their letter from Mrs. Granger. The letter was so full of kindness and concern that when the girls learned that they could visit Pennsylvania if they liked, they immediately accepted. Marigold was a little worried about traveling by train — remembering her only other train ride, when she and Tansy had been lost. But the news that Crystal and Ben would be their companions banished the child's fears.

Still, Elsie's advice had been wise. As Vi was preparing for bed that night, Tansy knocked at her door.

"May I ask you something, Miss Vi?" she inquired.

"Anything you like," Vi said, motioning the girl to come and sit beside her on the bed. "I may not have the answer, but I will try."

"I was wondering if…" Tansy started hesitantly, "if this trip means we will be leaving you and Samaritan House."

Vi sat up and took Tansy in her embrace. "It's only a visit," she said. "It's a chance to meet your family and know how much they love you. But you will be coming back to us. I promise."

"That's good," Tansy said in a near-whisper. "I want to know my Daddy's family. Really I do. But I don't want to leave you and Mrs. O and Polly or anybody here. It would be like finding something beautiful and then losing it."

"You'll never lose us, Tansy," Vi said. "Even if you decide that you want to live with your grandparents someday, you'll always have us. You and Marigold are part of our family, our Samaritan family, and we all love each other. Though we aren't relatives, we're like sisters and brothers, aren't we?"

"That's how I feel," Tansy said. "Like you and Miss Emily are big sisters and Dr. Bowman is a big brother and Polly is my little sister."

"What of Mrs. O and Christine and Enoch and Mrs. Appleton?" Vi asked.

Tansy looked up into her face and smiled. "Oh, they're aunts and uncles—really kind and good aunts and uncles. Mr. Fredericks too. Oh, we almost forgot Jacob. He's practically our baby brother."

Vi hugged her and rocked her in a playful way. "We are a family, and when you come back from Pennsylvania, you'll tell us about your grandparents and your aunt. And we'll think of them as family, too. Do you have the answer to your question now?" Vi said into Tansy's ear.

"Yes, ma'am," Tansy said. "And I do want to go to Pennsylvania."

"Well, I'm glad of that," Vi said cheerfully, "for you're going to have a very good time with your family and Crystal and Ben."

She loosened her arms, and Tansy hopped down from the bed. "Thank you for talking with me," Tansy said. "I know it will be good now, because I know I can come home to Samaritan House."

"Always," Vi said, bending to kiss Tansy's forehead.

A flurry of telegrams were sent back and forth between India Bay and Philadelphia, as arrangements were made

for the girls' trip. A week later, Vi and Mrs. O'Flaherty accompanied the girls, Crystal, and Ben to the railroad station. Vi's Uncle Edward Allison would be meeting them in Philadelphia, and he had organized the final leg of their journey to the Evanses' home. Tansy and Marigold were excited to begin their trip, but as the train left the station, Vi remarked how much she would miss the children during the next three weeks.

"None of us will miss the girls nearly as much as Polly will," Mrs. O'Flaherty said, as they walked away from the platform. "She will need some extra attention if she is not to become too lonely. I'm planning several excursions for her while the other girls are away. I think this is an opportune time to show her the museum and the new library. Polly has never been outside of Wildwood that she remembers."

"Is she making good progress?" Vi asked.

"Indeed," Mrs. O'Flaherty said proudly. "Polly is a quiet child, but I have discovered that she is very imaginative. She makes up the most delightful stories to entertain Tansy and Marigold. And you should take a look at her drawings. It is hard to judge the work of a six-year-old, but I believe she may have some talent."

"Really?" Vi asked. "I'd like to see her drawings."

"She would be very pleased by your interest," Mrs. O'Flaherty replied. "I don't think you know how much all the girls look up to you, Vi, and to Emily and our Zoe. In their eyes, you are very modern and capable young ladies."

They had just left the station and reached their carriage. Vi was laughing as she helped Mrs. O'Flaherty into the carriage. Then she paid the boy who was minding the vehicle, and she climbed up to the driver's seat to take the reins.

Calling down to her friend, she said, "I don't think of myself as 'modern.' A little capable perhaps, but not modern."

Turning to the task at hand, she gently snapped the reins and guided the horse into the crowded street.

Even amid all the hustle and bustle of the clinic, the school, and the new home visiting service, the residents of Samaritan House keenly felt the absence of Tansy and Marigold. Young Polly was especially quiet, so Vi made a point of asking the child about her drawings, and Polly perked up considerably as she displayed her pictures for "Miss Vi."

Asked to talk about her drawings, Polly had a story for each one. There were a number of colorful pictures of the mission cat, Jam, and for each picture, Polly had an adventure: Jam climbing into the Christmas tree and falling sleeping on a snowflake. Jam finding a mouse in the pantry and making friends with it.

"I like your pictures very much," Vi said, earning one of Polly's pretty smiles. "And you have such good stories for each one. Do you enjoy making up pretend stories?"

"Yes, Miss Vi," Polly said. "I like making up things in my head. Mama says I'm her little dreamer 'cause I dream up things. Do you think that's bad, Miss Vi?"

"Not at all, so long as you know the difference between what is true and what is make-believe. Imagination is one of God's gifts to us, and He trusts us to use it for good purposes," Vi said. Then she asked, "Could I draw with you sometime, Polly? I like to draw very much, but I haven't had much time for it lately."

Polly's eyes widened with delight as she said, "Would you, Miss Vi? Would you help me make better pictures?"

"I think your pictures are just fine," Vi said with a warm smile. "Maybe you could tell me some more of your stories. I think they're very exciting."

"They're just for fun," Polly said in an embarrassed way. Then the child's expression changed, and Vi saw sadness in her little face.

"I'm missing Marigold and Tansy," Polly said. "I've never had friends like them."

"I know that they are missing you too," Vi responded. But she added in a bright tone, "We shan't be lonely for long. Miss Zoe is coming tomorrow and will stay through the weekend. Would you show her your drawings, Polly? Miss Zoe is one of the most imaginative people I know."

"Is Miss Zoe your good-est friend?" Polly asked.

Vi said, "She is one of my closest friends. But I couldn't pick just one person, for there are so many people whom I love and admire—including you and your mother, and Mrs. O and Miss Emily and…"

"And Jesus," Polly said matter-of-factly. "You love Him a lot."

"Yes, I do," Vi said with a warm smile. "He is my very best friend."

"Mine too," Polly agreed.

Ed brought Zoe to the mission the next afternoon. He carried her bag inside, but when Vi asked him to stay, Ed said that he had an important business appointment.

Violet's Perplexing Puzzles

"But you'll return for supper, won't you?" Vi asked.

"I really can't, for my meeting will extend through dinner," Ed replied. "May I come tomorrow night?"

"Of course you may. But what is this business that is more important than your sister?" she teased.

"Something I've been working on for a while," he replied with a mysterious smile. "If all goes well, I will tell you about it tomorrow."

In a good-natured way, Vi chided her brother about arousing her curiosity. But Ed was in such a hurry to get to his meeting that Vi had no chance to ask the one question that had come to dominate her mind. Only a week remained in the month of January, and yet she had heard nothing from Mark Raymond since before Christmas. Had the professor decided not to visit India Bay after all? Surely, she believed, Ed would know, but now she must wait another day to pose her question.

As Vi accompanied Zoe upstairs, she questioned her friend about Ed's business.

"I know little more than you," Zoe said, "except that whatever it is, it has put Ed in a cheerful frame of mind. We had an interesting conversation during the drive here, and your brother did not once accuse me of being 'girlish' as he does so often. Ed is such a confusing person. I never know what he is thinking."

"You've said that he has some of Grandpapa's strictness, and you're right," Vi observed. "But he also has much of Papa's way too. Ed can be very witty, and in many ways he's quite advanced in his thinking."

"Well, he certainly confuses me," Zoe said as they reached the third floor landing. "Just when I expect him to be pompous and condescending to me, he turns around and treats me as a peer—as he did this morning. Really, Vi, that brother of yours is a mystery. Trying to understand him makes my head swim at times!"

"I wonder you bother to try," Vi said playfully, "for he can be beastly to us young ladies."

Zoe turned to stare at Vi. "Beastly?" she said in a serious tone. "Oh, I wouldn't say that at all. He's always kind to me—to everyone. It's when he treats me as a child that I get upset with him," she added with a sigh. "I'm young, but not a child."

"I think Ed knows that," Vi said. She did not express the second half of her thought: *but he is not quite ready to admit it to himself.*

Zoe was soon unpacked and settling into the routine of Samaritan House. She volunteered to help Mary in the kitchen and then—at Vi's request—to visit with Polly and look at the child's drawings. Nothing more was said about Ed or his mysterious business.

Despite their awareness that Samaritan House was always open to anyone in need, the people of Wildwood were generally conscientious about not disturbing the residents at night. The people of the community understood, better than most, the meaning of long hours of hard work and the need for rest. Apart from emergencies, they were inclined to stay away in the evenings, and the people of Samaritan House valued this show of respect from their neighbors.

So after supper that night, Vi availed herself of the quiet time and retreated to her office to catch up on her personal

correspondence. She was writing a letter to one of her friends in Ohio when Zoe interrupted her.

"There's a man I've never seen before at the front door. He asks to speak to you," Zoe said. "He's not exactly like most of the people who come here. He's well dressed in a flashy way."

"Did he give his name?" Vi asked.

"Clink or Clinch, I think," Zoe replied.

At the name, Vi's expression instantly darkened. Even in the soft light of the oil lamp, Zoe could see the flash in Vi's eyes.

"Should I send him away?" Zoe asked with concern.

Vi, her brow furrowed with thought, said after several moments, "No, I will see him. I'll go to the door. Will you ask Mrs. O to come to the meeting room? I'd like you both to join me."

Zoe hurried away to find Mrs. O'Flaherty. Vi slowly removed her spectacles and laid them on her desk. She carefully corked the ink bottle and then wiped the nib of her writing pen with a soft cloth. She was hardly conscious of any of her movements, for her mind was full of questions: *What could he want with me? Why come at night? Could this have anything to do with Tansy and Marigold?*

Shaking her head as if to dash away her questions, Vi stood. She squared her shoulders and almost marched from the room, like a soldier going into battle. She had seen Mr. Clinch on a couple of occasions, but she had never met him. *Does he come here as friend or foe?*

Whatever his motives, Vi reminded herself to be polite. *But not too polite*, she told herself as she walked into the entry hall where he was standing near the front door.

Clinch removed his hat as he saw Vi approaching. He smiled, and Vi was taken aback somewhat, for his smile seemed genuinely friendly.

"Miss Travilla?" he said in a questioning way—as if he did not know exactly who she was.

At her nod, he continued, "I am Tobias Clinch, owner of the Wildwood Hotel. I apologize for not introducing myself earlier, but I understand how busy you have been getting this mission on its feet. One of my customers told me that you sometimes receive callers in the evenings, but if I am intruding…"

"Samaritan House is always open," Vi said. Hearing the primness of her tone, she added more graciously, "Please join us in the meeting room. It also serves as a parlor for guests."

Mr. Clinch placed his overcoat and hat on the hall stand, and followed Vi to the next room. Mrs. O'Flaherty and Zoe, who had come down the back stairs and through the kitchen, were already seated. Vi made the introductions and then motioned Mr. Clinch to a comfortable chair near the fireplace. She considered offering him coffee but decided not to; she wanted to know the reason for Mr. Clinch's visit first.

After complimenting the work that had been done on the house, Mr. Clinch made a statement Vi hadn't anticipated.

"I have come to ask for your help," he said. "I have a problem on my hands, and I am unable to resolve it. I thought that ladies such as yourselves might be able to assist me."

"We shall do what we can," Vi said, keeping her voice calm. "Whether we can be of help remains to be seen. But what is this problem?"

Violet's Perplexing Puzzles

Mr. Clinch sat a bit forward in his chair and said, "It is not a *what*, Miss Travilla, but a *who*. Sometime back, I lost my cook at the hotel. I believe that she now works for you—Mrs. Appleton, Mary Appleton?"

"Yes, she does," Vi replied, her tone more natural now, for his statement had gotten her interest. "Your loss was our gain, for Mrs. Appleton is a splendid cook."

"She was not easy to replace," Mr. Clinch went on, lowering his eyes for a moment. Looking up at Vi again, he continued, "I did hire someone several weeks ago, and she is the problem. Her name is Alma Hansen, and she is a recent arrival in our country from Germany. Her cooking is satisfactory, but her English is very poor. As you can guess, we do not communicate well."

He smiled, and once again, Vi had the impression that the smile was genuine.

"Miss Hansen's a hard worker," he went on, "but she's unhappy. She cries constantly and seems frightened of her own shadow. I'm afraid she is making herself sick. I speak a little German, and I've tried to find out what is wrong, but I can't make heads or tails of what she says. I thought perhaps one of you ladies, being so well educated, might know her language and could help her."

"Do you wish to keep her on as your cook?" Mrs. O'Flaherty asked.

"Only if she wants to stay," Mr. Clinch replied. "I run a hotel, ma'am, and it's not good for my business to have an employee who is always tearful and depressed. It makes my guests unhappy."

"You could let her go," Mrs. O'Flaherty noted.

Mr. Clinch smiled again and said, "In spite of what you've probably heard, I'm not a heartless man. I thought about firing her, but I just couldn't do it. She's a nice kid—

ah, young lady—and all alone in this country. If I had a daughter, I'd hope someone would be looking out for her well-being. I'm at my wit's end, ladies, and that's why I've come to seek your advice."

"Could you find another cook for the hotel?" Vi asked.

"Maybe not one as good as Mary Appleton, but yes, I could replace Miss Hansen quick enough," he said. "It's Miss Hansen who worries me. I can't see myself just tossing her out. I mean, ma'am, where would she go? On her own, she might fall afoul of dangers she knows nothing about. I don't want to go into details, but there's a lot of evil in this city. And she's as innocent as a lamb."

As he spoke, a look of deep concern had come to his face. "She needs a family to take care of her," he said in a soft tone. "That's what made me think of you ladies."

He lowered his eyes again, as if what he was saying were hard for him. Then he added, "I've heard good things about your mission and how you're helping people. I want to do what's right for Miss Hansen. I really do. I was thinking that maybe if you met her, you might be able to tell me what to do for her."

Several moments of silence went by; then Vi asked, "Can you bring her here? We will be better able to judge the situation after we meet her. Mrs. O'Flaherty is fluent in German, and Miss Love and I both speak the language. We could at least communicate."

Mr. Clinch looked up, his smile seeming to convey both hope and gratitude. "I'd be most appreciative, Miss Travilla. I can bring her tomorrow if you want."

Vi rose from her seat and said, "That would be fine, Mr. Clinch. About nine-thirty in the morning, if you can spare Miss Hansen from your kitchen."

Violet's Perplexing Puzzles

Mr. Clinch stood quickly, saying, "I'm more concerned about that girl than her cooking. I'll have her here. Thank you, all of you. This will be a weight off my mind. Now, I must go. It's been very pleasant to meet you."

He bowed slightly to Mrs. O'Flaherty and Zoe, and Vi showed him to the door. Then she hurried back to her friends.

"Did you believe any of that?" she asked.

"About the girl, yes," Mrs. O'Flaherty said. "As for the rest of what he said, not a word."

"But he seemed so sincere," Zoe said.

Mrs. O'Flaherty replied, "He was quite good at acting the part of the worried employer, but our past experience tells me something very different."

Vi sat down again and said, "It is strange to have met Mr. Clinch at last. We shall never know exactly what part he played in the attempt to kidnap Tansy and Marigold and the assault on Enoch. We have no real evidence that he was behind the efforts to drive the mission out of Wildwood. Perhaps we assumed too easily that he is a villain. Even so, I do not trust him, Mrs. O. Yet I don't want to leap to conclusions. Zoe may be right. In this matter, he may be entirely sincere. On the other hand…"

She paused, and Mrs. O'Flaherty said, "In this case, we may be dealing with a wolf in sheep's clothing. Whatever his true motive in asking for our help, I do not believe that this young German woman's welfare is a real worry for him."

"Then we must do all we can to help her," Vi said firmly.

Zoe, whose nature was to give the benefit of the doubt, returned to her first thought. "Is it not possible that the man's concern is real?"

"All things are possible," Mrs. O'Flaherty replied with a hearty laugh. "Pigs may fly and leopards may change their spots. I don't expect to see it happen, but you remind me, Zoe, not to be so close-minded. It is a fault that grows worse with age."

Vi let out a big sigh. "Well, I don't know what to think of Mr. Clinch, except that I am sure this situation is more complicated than it appears. With that charming smile of his, Mr. Clinch had me almost believing him at times. Dear me, what a puzzle some people are!"

There was no puzzlement in the mind of Tobias Clinch as he walked the dark street back to his hotel. He knew that the ladies were at that moment discussing him—trying to decide whether his request for assistance was real or false. And that was just what he wanted.

They'll be debating everything I said, he thought with a twisted pleasure. *The Irish woman will size me up as a fraud. The young one will want to think the best of me. But what are you thinking, Miss Violet Travilla? The Bible tells you to love your neighbor, and that's what you will try to do—no matter how strong your instinct that I'm not what I seemed to be tonight. That's how I will win our little war. I can make you doubt yourself by making others doubt you. I'll turn your strengths into weaknesses. It will be easy now that I have my foot in the mission door, thanks to that German girl.* His musings turned to Alma Hansen: *If those women can dry up your endless flood of tears and misery, Alma, then well and good for them. But you are mine to control, you silly girl, and you'll do what I tell you. You haven't any choice, have you?*

Violet's Perplexing Puzzles

Clinch was very happy with himself when he entered the hotel. Tinkling music poured from the piano in the saloon, but there were not so many customers at the bar as there had always been before the mission opened. Not so many men at the gambling tables in the rear of the saloon. Usually this situation infuriated him. But not tonight. He had come up with a plan to protect his business and regain his absolute control of Wildwood.

Ever since the December night when he had spied on Vi at the ball at the Lansings' home, he had secretly studied her habits and those of the other residents of the mission. In the most subtle and seemingly innocent way, he'd questioned the people of Wildwood about the young mission lady and her friends—all to learn as much as he could about their vulnerabilities. Then he'd plotted carefully, and tonight, he had set his plan in motion.

Having met Violet Travilla at last, he almost felt sorry for her. *She's suspicious of me*, he thought. *She's no fool, but she's too kind for her own good. Her open heart will be her downfall.*

The idea made him smile as he entered his office, but it was not an attractive sight—and nothing like the smile that he used to charm the ladies of Samaritan House.

Fraulein Alma

He brought me out into a spacious place; he rescued me because he delighted in me.

2 SAMUEL 22:20

Fraulein Alma

*M*r. Clinch took Alma Hansen to the mission the next morning. He'd had a talk with the young woman before they left the hotel, and he was confident she would follow his every instruction to the letter.

Mrs. O'Flaherty met the hotel owner and Miss Hansen at the door of Samaritan House. Mr. Clinch said he would return in an hour to get his cook, but Mrs. O'Flaherty insisted that someone from the mission would escort her back to the hotel. After briskly bidding Mr. Clinch farewell, Mrs. O'Flaherty welcomed Miss Hansen and brought her inside. As she took the visitor's cloak, Mrs. O noticed that the girl was trembling, so she showed her into the meeting room where a cheerful fire added to the warmth of the large room.

Miss Hansen said barely a word, but she seemed pleased to hear her native language, which Mrs. O'Flaherty spoke extremely well. Mrs. O's first impression was of a shy and unusually nervous young person—about seventeen years old, she guessed. Miss Hansen was dressed plainly, but Mrs. O'Flaherty noticed that her clothing was finely made. The girl was very pale, and her soft brown eyes were rimmed with red, as if she had recently been crying. She was a tall girl, almost as tall as Mrs. O'Flaherty, and painfully thin. Mrs. O'Flaherty wondered if she might be ill.

Miss Hansen took a seat near the fire, and she gratefully thanked Mrs. O'Flaherty for the offer of tea. Leaving her for a few minutes, Mrs. O went to the kitchen to ask Mary to brew a pot and then hurried to the mission office to get Vi.

Violet's Perplexing Puzzles

Returning to the meeting room, Mrs. O'Flaherty introduced Vi to *Fraulein* Hansen, and both of the mission ladies made small talk in German until Mary came in with the tea. Vi and Mrs. O'Flaherty had already decided not to question the young woman at first. In her work at the mission, Vi had observed that questioning too closely often made strangers ill at ease.

"We are very glad to have you visit our mission," Vi said in her serviceable German. "Like you, we are new to Wildwood. Our mission has been open for just a few months, but we have made many friends already."

The girl looked down at the cup and saucer she held, and said softly in German, "It is good to make friends. I have friends at home, in Germany, but not in America."

"I hope we shall become friends," Vi said in the German language. "I hope you will visit us often."

Miss Hansen looked up suddenly and asked, "May I?"

"Anytime you like," Vi said with her warmest smile. Then she ventured a questioning remark: "Mr. Clinch tells us that you cook at the hotel."

"Yes, but cooking is not my best occupation. At home, I sew. I am a seamstress."

Saying this seemed to relax the girl, so Mrs. O'Flaherty asked more questions about her work. Miss Hansen told them that she had been taught sewing by her mother and grandmother and then, before coming to America, she had trained in the workshop of a dressmaker in the city of Cologne.

"It is my ambition to have my own dress shop someday, but I fear that it will not be," Miss Hansen said in a sorrowful way.

"Perhaps we can help," Vi said.

Fraulein Alma

Vi had planned only to meet with the young woman. She had no intention of taking action until she knew a good deal more about Miss Hansen, but something about Alma touched her deeply. Perhaps it was the pain in the girl's eyes. Perhaps it was the joy in her voice when she talked of learning to sew at her mother's knee—joy that broke through her sadness for a few minutes, like a ray of sunlight that suddenly penetrates a stormy sky.

Whatever the cause, Vi felt herself compelled to do something quickly. It meant acting on an impulse, but seeing Miss Hansen's fragile emotions, Vi didn't want the girl to suffer a minute longer than necessary. Besides, Vi had an idea.

"We have a growing collection of clothing for people in need," Vi began, "but most of the items must be repaired before they can be given away. We've done what we can, but none of us here have the time or the talent for such work. It would not be like having your own shop, but at least it would not be cooking. And we truly do need your skills. Would you come here to work?"

"Do you mean you would employ me to sew?" Miss Hansen asked incredulously.

"Yes, I do mean that," Vi said, also a little surprised by her sudden offer.

"It is a very good idea," Mrs. O'Flaherty said with a grin. "And there is an empty bedroom in our living quarters where you could live if you like."

"It would be so good," Miss Hansen said in a choked voice. "This is the first time I have been able to speak of myself in my own language. I understand Mr. Clinch when he tells me what to do, but I cannot tell him of my unhappy feelings. But you understand me. I will be a very good worker. I will make you no problems."

"Then you will come here?" Vi asked.

"I must ask Mr. Clinch," Miss Hansen said, lowering her head. "He may not permit me to leave."

"Let me speak with him," Vi said. "Mrs. O'Flaherty and I will go back to the hotel with you, and I feel confident that you will spend your first night at Samaritan House this very evening."

And so it happened. The three women went to the hotel in the carriage. Mrs. O'Flaherty helped Alma pack her things while Vi saw Mr. Clinch. He agreed to the arrangement and confided that he had already found a replacement cook. His only request was a brief private meeting with Alma—to pay her final wages, he said—while his clerk loaded the luggage in Vi's buggy.

Everything was accomplished so quickly that Alma was almost dizzy. Mr. Clinch had let her leave on the condition that she return to see him on certain days and report on her progress. He had been very cordial when he took her to his office and counted out her pay from his money box. He had given her an extra ten dollars, and Alma began to regret being suspicious of him. He had taken her to the mission, hadn't he? And the ten dollars was a generous gift, wasn't it? All he wanted in return was that she keep a few secrets; if she could do that, he said, he would help her again, with a much more important matter. She did not know why he insisted on the secrets, but she owed him this debt of gratitude. She would do as Mr. Clinch asked—just as he knew she would.

Alma Hansen was introduced to the other mission residents and Emily Clayton at their lunch that day. Alma understood little of what they said and depended on Mrs. O'Flaherty to translate for her. But from their open and friendly expressions, Alma knew that she was truly welcome in this house. She was especially taken by Zoe, who was close to her age and who chatted with her gaily in fair German. It quickly became clear that they had much in common, for Zoe had also come to America from Europe and was very interested in all things related to dressmaking.

After lunch, Vi and Zoe showed Alma the storage room, where most of the boxes of donated clothing remained unpacked. Alma and Zoe were soon opening the boxes and examining the contents.

"I thought you might wish to unpack your own things and perhaps enjoy a nap," Vi said, hoping that her German construction was correct.

"If it is permissible, Miss Travilla, I would like to work today," Alma replied shyly.

"And I'll help her," Zoe said with her usual enthusiasm. "We can at least see which items need repair. Then I can help Miss Hansen to settle in."

Vi laughed pleasantly and said, "Well, then, I'll be helping Mary in the kitchen, if you need anything. I am so pleased you decided to join us in our work. There is but one request I have of you. Please call me Vi from now on. Within this house, we are all friends."

"And I am Alma," the young woman said with a sweet simplicity. "I am happy to be with friends, and I shall do my best to be a good friend to you all."

Vi was walking out the door, but she turned and spoke to Zoe, in English rather than German. "Don't forget that Ed is coming for supper tonight. He'll be here at eight."

"I haven't forgotten," Zoe replied. "I'm hoping he'll tell us about his mysterious business. You know how mysteries intrigue me."

Vi was smiling broadly as she closed the door, remembering all too well Zoe's fascination with mysteries.

⁓

Mrs. O'Flaherty and the others ate at their regular time that evening; then Mrs. O gave Alma a tour of the house and its facilities. Alma was amazed by the many services that Samaritan House provided and asked Mrs. O a number of questions. But after they had seen the clinic and the classroom, Mrs. O'Flaherty could tell that the young seamstress was weary and suggested an early bedtime.

"Would you like to share in my devotion tonight?" Mrs. O'Flaherty asked Alma in German. "I like to read some verses and discuss them before my prayers. Vi and I often have some of our best talks before bed."

Alma was very pleased by this invitation. "Thank you, Mrs. O'Flaherty," she replied in her native language. "I would like that. Before my mother died and my brother left for America, we would say our prayers together every night. I miss that very much."

Alma looked away to hide her tears. "I miss *them* very much," she added, the words catching in her throat.

Mrs. O'Flaherty was surprised at Alma's mention of a brother. But she did not want to upset the young woman with questions, so she said gently, "I know how hard it is to be away from family and the home in which one grew up. But the Lord will comfort you, dear girl. You are never alone with a Friend such as He. In this world and the one beyond, He will always give you refuge in the shelter of His wings."

Alma looked back and said, "Those words are from Psalm 61: 'I long to dwell in your tent forever and take refuge in the shelter of your wings.' That was one of my mother's favorites, and she often said that there is great comfort in the Psalms."

"Shall we take Psalm 61 as our text tonight?" Mrs. O'Flaherty asked. "If you have a Bible in your native language, perhaps you can read the Psalm to me."

"I have my mother's Bible. It is my most prized possession," Alma responded. Then a small smile touched her thin lips. "I would like to read to you, for I cannot cry when I concentrate on the hopeful words of my Heavenly Father."

"Then I will leave you to get your Bible and prepare for bed. I will be back in about ten minutes," Mrs. O'Flaherty said. She laid a strong hand on Alma's arm. "We shall read His Word and pray together, and then you can sleep well tonight, for His love and faithfulness are protecting you."

Downstairs, Vi and Zoe were bustling about in the kitchen. They had delayed eating and would have their supper with Ed. Mary Appleton had cooked for them, but Vi and Zoe refused to let her prepare the table and serve the meal. Evening was Mary's special time with her daughter, and Vi insisted that Mary abandon the kitchen to her.

Vi was putting together a vegetable salad and warming a pan of yeast rolls when Ed arrived. Zoe, who had just finished setting one of the tables in the meeting room, heard his knocking and went to the door.

Violet's Perplexing Puzzles

Zoe was smiling happily when she opened the door. She was eager to welcome Ed. But her mouth fell open in astonishment at what she saw. It was so unexpected that she could not speak for several moments.

Ed couldn't help laughing at the dazed look on her beautiful face.

"I do believe I have finally succeeded in rendering you speechless," he said as he entered.

"Is—is this your mysterious business?" Zoe managed to stammer out.

"The main part of it," Ed replied. "Where is Vi?"

"In the kitchen."

"Will you get her, Zoe?" Ed asked. "Say nothing of this, and we shall enjoy her reaction. I trust she will be as awestruck as you."

Zoe had regained her composure by now. "Oh, Vi will be most surprised," she said with a sparkling laugh.

Rushing toward the kitchen, she barged through the door and announced a little breathlessly, "Ed has arrived!"

Vi didn't look up from her work. She said that she was almost finished with her salad dressing and would be out to greet her brother in another few minutes.

"Well, hurry up," Zoe said impatiently. Then in an effort to conceal her excitement, she added, "That salad looks delicious. I hope Ed is hungry."

"Go on," Vi laughed, "and keep him entertained. He is our guest tonight."

"Our guest," Zoe said with a giggle. "Yes, he's our guest. It's so very nice to have guests, even when they are not invited."

Vi didn't have a chance to ask her friend the meaning of that last remark, for Zoe had left, closing the kitchen door firmly behind her.

CHAPTER

7

Who Could Have Imagined?

Now to him who is able to do immeasurably more than all we ask or imagine…

EPHESIANS 3:20

Who Could Have Imagined?

*V*i shook her head as she removed her apron and then checked her face in a small mirror that hung on the kitchen wall. *If I didn't know better, I would think that Zoe had not seen Ed for months — not a mere day,* she mused to herself as she wiped a spot of flour from her chin and pinned a stray strand of her glossy dark hair back in its place. *I wonder if Ed knows her feelings? Or Zoe his, for that matter? But it isn't my place to speculate. What is plain to me may not be so obvious to my brother and my friend. And who am I to judge their true feelings? I could be seeing romance where there is only friendship. Once again, I am probably leaping to conclusions.*

She turned from the mirror and quickly straightened her skirt as she tried to put her conjectures from her mind. But a line from a poem she had recently read popped unbidden into her head: "Youths green and happy in first love…"

She laughed at herself and her romantic notions and went to greet her brother.

Ed was standing with Zoe, near the front window. Vi walked up to him and kissed his cheek. "I trust your business is happily concluded," she said in a teasing way.

"Almost, little sister," he replied, "but there are some final details. In fact, I thought that you and Zoe might help me with a few questions that remain. I have brought my business with me tonight so that you might evaluate it for yourself."

He looked up, and his eyes seemed to fasten on something behind Vi.

Instinctively, she turned to glance in the same direction, and there in the doorway stood Professor Mark Raymond.

He was smiling his slightly lopsided smile and looking uncharacteristically embarrassed.

A gasp escaped Vi as he approached. Her surprise was indeed complete.

"This little charade was all your brother's idea," the professor said apologetically as he extended his hand to her. "I hope you will forgive my unannounced arrival on your doorstep."

Vi gave him her hand, which he shook gently.

"Of course, I forgive you, Professor Raymond," she said. "It is Ed I must reproach for keeping your presence here a secret."

"The secrecy is in part my fault," he said, "for the business Ed speaks of is mine."

Vi's face showed her puzzlement, so Ed began to explain. "Mark has been in meetings at India Bay University for the past two days. They want him here to teach. They've made an extraordinary offer, and I hope you and Zoe will help me convince my friend to accept it."

Mark Raymond? Living and teaching in India Bay? The prospect stunned Vi. *How had this happened? Was it really possible?* She struggled with a confusion of questions. Zoe and Ed were saying something, but their words were lost to her.

After what seemed a long, long time—but was in reality a matter of mere seconds—she said, "Well, come everyone and be seated. Professor Raymond, this is extraordinary news, and you must tell us all about it."

That her voice was calm and clear surprised her almost as much as the professor's presence in her mission, for she did not feel at all calm inside.

"Now you must tell us absolutely everything," Zoe said as they settled into the comfortable chairs clustered around the fireplace.

Who Could Have Imagined?

"It was Ed who started it all," the professor said. "Last fall, during my first visit to Ion, he introduced me to some of his friends on the faculty at India Bay University. We visited the campus, and I met the head of the classics department—a man whose scholarship I have long admired. As it happens, Professor Kincaid is retiring at the end of the spring term, and he asked me to suggest possible replacements. We had a number of discussions—he is a delightful man, by the way—and I gave him my recommendations. I thought that was the end of it, but when I returned here in December, I was approached by the president of the University. It was on the night of Dr. and Mrs. Lansing's ball, Miss Travilla. The president wanted to meet with me the next day, and in that meeting, he raised the subject of my coming to India Bay and taking the leadership of the classical languages department when Professor Kincaid retires. He is also interested in starting an archaeology curriculum, for which I would be responsible. Now an offer is on the table, and I must make my decision."

"This is so exciting!" Zoe exclaimed. "You will accept, won't you?"

"I am inclined to," the professor said, "but there are a number of things to consider."

"That's why I asked Mark to join us this evening," Ed said with a grin. "I want us to help him *consider* his choice by extolling the virtues of India Bay, the University, life in the South…"

He hesitated, and Professor Raymond said, "I do not doubt that everything you mention is wonderful. But, my friend, I didn't accept your invitation tonight in order to talk about myself. In truth, I was anxious to see Miss Travilla and Miss Love again and catch up on the news of

Samaritan House. But someone is missing. I expected to see Mrs. O'Flaherty. I hope she is well."

"Quite well," Vi said assuringly. "She simply retired early. We've had a busy day."

A look of concern registered on the professor's face. He said, "And I am intruding on your hospitality."

"Oh, not at all!" Vi declared. "Zoe and I have been looking forward to our supper tonight, and we are so glad that you will join us. I propose that we dine now and continue our conversation at the table."

She stood, and the others also rose. "If you gentlemen will be seated," she said with a dimpled smile, "Zoe and I will serve."

"Don't tell me that you cooked, little sister?" Ed asked jokingly.

"Would you be afraid to eat my cooking, big brother?" she retorted in a sprightly manner. Then she said, "Have no fear. The meal was prepared for us by Mrs. Appleton, and I know that you admire her cuisine."

The men took their places at one of the long dining tables, at which Zoe had already placed an extra setting when Vi was not looking. The young ladies vanished into the kitchen and soon returned with the first course. At Vi's request, Ed said grace.

The discussion was convivial as the meal proceeded. Vi told the gentlemen about Alma Hansen's arrival. Then the professor asked about Tansy and Marigold, and Vi provided a thorough updating of their situation.

"I'm so glad you located their family," the professor said. "I am sorry I didn't see the girls on my last visit, but now you know the reason—my meeting with the University president."

Ed asked, "Will you bring your children with you, if you accept the University's offer?"

The professor hesitated for a moment; then he said, "I would have to find a house and someone to care for them when I am at work or away. I don't know…"

He paused, and Zoe jumped in, saying, "We could help you, Professor. I know Vi's Mamma would be glad to help. Wouldn't she, Vi?"

"She would," Vi said, "and gladly."

She was remembering the professor's letter to her, and she had an idea that finding a house and someone to look after his children was not his main concern. She sensed the discomfort in his hesitancy to speak of his son and daughters, so she steered the conversation in another direction.

"Our school is off to a good start," she said. "I am impressed with the warm style of our new teacher, Mr. Fredericks. I imagine his style of teaching is not unlike your own, Professor."

"I have little experience teaching young children," he said. Vi heard a trace of wistfulness in his voice, and she realized he was not referring to the classroom. *He is thinking of his own children*, she thought, and her heart went out to him.

The professor spoke again, this time in the cool and slightly stodgy tone that had so annoyed Vi when they first met. "If Mr. Fredericks believes that challenging discussion between teacher and student is essential to learning, then yes, perhaps our styles are similar."

"Maybe you can meet him while you're here," Ed said. "He's an interesting fellow, and my brothers say he's a great favorite at the Boys' Academy."

"That means you must visit the mission again," Zoe added in her bubbly way. "You should really come during the day, Professor, so you can see the mission at work."

"I'd like that," Professor Raymond replied, casting a look at Vi.

"We shall probably give you a job to do," Vi said with a smile.

"A small price for the opportunity to observe your work and meet Mr. Fredericks," the professor said.

"You could come tomorrow," Zoe said gaily. "Tomorrow is Friday and Dr. Bowman will be here, too. He'd be so glad to see —"

"Zoe!" Ed snapped, cutting her off. "Mark may have plans, and Vi as well. *They* are the ones to make the arrangements for a visit."

Ed stopped himself before he said, *not you*. He instantly regretted the sharpness of his tone. But Zoe was always so impetuous! Her enthusiasm was one of her most endearing qualities, but sometimes she got carried away, and he simply felt it was his duty to correct her. He hadn't meant to hurt her feelings.

Seeing Zoe's face pale at Ed's curt remark, Vi quickly said, "Tomorrow would be perfect for us, Professor Raymond, if your schedule permits a visit."

"It does, Miss Travilla," Professor Raymond replied. "I am obliged to Miss Love for her suggestion."

He smiled so winningly at Zoe that her cheeks flushed pink and her eyes lit up with pleasure. "I made the suggestion for selfish reasons," she said. "I must return to The Oaks on Sunday, for I have some important lessons to attend to. If you come tomorrow, I will be able to see you again, Professor."

Who Could Have Imagined?

This began some discussion of the subjects that Zoe was studying with Horace Dinsmore, her guardian and teacher. As Zoe answered the professor's questions about her academic interests, Vi noticed that her brother was silent. There was a stormy look in Ed's dark eyes.

She'd seen the look before, whenever her brother was angry or frustrated with Zoe. Now she sensed that the look was different. Ed was not directing his anger at Zoe. His burning gaze seemed directed inward—as if he were staring reproachfully at himself. *My dear, sweet brother*, Vi thought. *My heart aches for you. I know that look—the shame you feel. I wish I could help you. I wish I knew how you could break through that reserve of yours and admit your true feelings to yourself. But there is One who will help you. Turn to Him. Trust Him.*

At last, Ed lowered his eyes. He pretended to go back to his meal, though in fact he merely moved the food about on his plate and ate nothing. In another few minutes, he picked up the thread of the professor and Zoe's conversation and entered in as if nothing had occurred.

But Vi knew that something had happened—something much larger than a momentary flare of temper between her brother and her dear friend.

Ed and Mark Raymond departed soon after supper was finished. Ed was staying the night at the Bayview Hotel, where the professor was in residence, and would return to Ion early the next morning. Vi asked the professor to come to the mission for breakfast so he could meet the other members of the staff before the workday began. The professor, who was an early riser, readily agreed.

Violet's Perplexing Puzzles

It was nearly eleven o'clock when the gentlemen left, and Vi and Zoe hurried to the kitchen to wash the dishes.

"I'm sorry, Vi," Zoe said as she brought the dirty plates to the sink. "I shouldn't have invited the professor to visit without consulting you."

"I'm glad you did," Vi replied sincerely. "You merely anticipated me by a few moments, for I intended to ask the same."

"It wasn't my place, and Ed was right to correct me," Zoe said, and Vi heard the break in her friend's voice. "But why did he have to do it so—so—publicly? As if I were an unruly child doing some mischief?"

Vi slipped the dishes carefully into the soapy water. "I don't know why exactly," she said slowly, "but I can tell you that he was ashamed of himself. Does it matter so much to you?"

Zoe laid a serving dish down beside the sink. She went to the kitchen table, slumped into a chair, and began to cry softly. Vi quickly dried her hands and came to sit beside her friend.

"It *does* matter," Zoe said in trembling tones. "It shouldn't, but it does matter. I don't want to embarrass Ed. Not ever. But I always seem to say the wrong thing when I am around him."

"You did not say anything wrong," Vi insisted firmly. "Ed was wrong to snap at you, and he knew it. He can be overly proud, and he is sometimes slow to admit his mistakes."

Zoe had taken a handkerchief from her sleeve and was dabbing at her eyes. A little smile tugged at her mouth as she said, "Uncle Horace has told me about the 'Dinsmore pride.' If I didn't care about Ed, I wouldn't care about his stupid pride. But—but—"

"But you do care," Vi said gently. "I think you care very much."

Who Could Have Imagined?

Zoe didn't respond at first. She blew her nose, rather loudly for so small a girl, and straightened her back. Then she shook her head, dislodging some of her blonde curls, and said with defiance, "Yes I do care about Ed, as I care about all of you. I just wish he would joke with me as he does with you. He's not my father, you know."

"I do know," Vi replied in a steady tone. "Ed can be annoying, though he usually has the best of motives."

"Perhaps I should correct *him* in front of others, and then he might understand how I feel," Zoe declared as she stood up and went purposefully back to the sink. "But I am not going to worry about him anymore. There are plenty of young men who have a higher opinion of me than your brother does."

She picked up the biscuit pan and began to scrub at it furiously.

Hoping to change the subject, Vi said in a light way, "Mamma told me that you have been enjoying a number of social outings of late. She says that you are the belle of the ball at all the young people's parties."

In spite of herself, Zoe laughed. "Don't you start teasing me, Vi," she said.

"I'm not. Really, I'm not," Vi protested. "Mamma meant what she said as a compliment, and she thinks Grand-mamma and Grandpapa are very happy that you are not spending all your time buried in your studies."

"Your grandmother wants to have a dinner dance in the spring," Zoe said in something very close to her normal buoyant tone.

They talked of many things (except Ed) while they finished the dishes. Vi asked about the parties that Zoe had attended, and Zoe told her about the doings of their mutual friends in the country—young people whom Vi did not often see since her move to Wildwood.

"They all ask about you, Vi," Zoe said. "They miss you."

"And I miss them," Vi said sincerely. "But I count on you to tell me what is going on with our friends."

"Well, I have a few bits of news you may not know," Zoe said with a sly smile. "Flossie Benham is engaged to Gerald Stokes, and Charles Lawrence is formally courting your friend Lillian Howard. I expect they will be engaged after Charles finishes his degree at India Bay University."

Zoe went on to give Vi details of several other romances blossoming among the young women and men of their acquaintance.

"I guess we have reached an age when weddings will be our main social activity," Vi observed.

Talking had made their work go quickly, and with the last of the clean dishes put away, Vi conducted a quick inspection of the kitchen, checked that the door and windows were securely locked, turned down the lamps, and took up a small lantern to light their way.

"Do you ever think about getting married?" Zoe asked as they climbed the narrow back stairs.

"Sometimes," Vi said. "But I'm not sure marriage is for me, at least not for a long time. The mission would leave me little time for a husband and family."

"Aren't you afraid of becoming an old maid?" Zoe said.

"Not at all," Vi said firmly. "I might marry someday, if I find someone I truly love. Yet that might not happen, and there's nothing wrong with being a single woman, is there? There are many accomplished women who remain single—like Florence Nightingale and Clara Barton and Louisa May Alcott and—"

Who Could Have Imagined?

"And our friend Dr. Frazier in New York," Zoe broke in. "You're right, Vi. No one should get married just to be married. That would be the opposite of love, for it would be only for personal benefit. But if a person really and truly loves another person with all her heart…"

Her words trailed off just as they reached the third floor. They walked toward Zoe's bedroom. Zoe was about to say good night when Vi put her hand gently on her friend's arm.

"I hope you won't worry too much about what Ed said," she began. "Try to be patient with him, even when he's impatient with you. Talking about marriage and our friends' romances, well, it makes me think. You and I and Ed are at a time in our lives when everything seems to be changing for us. We're grown now. It is our time to 'put childish ways behind….' But we are inexperienced at being adults, and we're bound to make mistakes."

Zoe, her expression serious, nodded her head in agreement and said, "I know, Vi. Being an adult means taking responsibility for ourselves. We've been preparing for this time all our lives, but it can be scary."

"We know that God is guiding us," Vi said, "but I think that He also wants us to be understanding of one another. Even strong young men like Ed can sometimes be unsure of themselves."

"And strong young women like you and me must sometimes put our own pride aside and forgive," Zoe said with a gentle smile. "I am too quick to defend myself when Ed teases and corrects me."

"And my brother can be too quick to tease and correct," Vi responded. "but he regrets his errors almost as soon as he makes them. I'm sure he will apologize to you for his behavior tonight. I just can't tell you how or when."

Violet's Perplexing Puzzles

"Ed is an enigma," Zoe said with a soft laugh. "Another mystery to solve. And you are right that I must be patient. I will work on it, Vi, though patience is not one of my strengths, as you know. And even if Ed doesn't apologize, I will be forgiving."

"Forgiveness is one of your great strengths," Vi said. "That, and your skills as a detective," she added with a chuckle as the two friends parted for the night.

CHAPTER

8

Making an Impression

*She opens her arms to the
poor and extends her
hands to the needy.*

PROVERBS 31:20

Making an Impression

*M*ark Raymond arrived the next morning just as the mission residents were about to begin their breakfast. Mrs. O'Flaherty met him at the door and ushered him inside. She noticed that under his arm, he carried a white box tied with string. But as he did not volunteer an explanation of the package, she didn't ask about it.

In the dining area, Zoe and the others were seated, and Zoe broke into a beautiful smile when she saw him.

"Professor Raymond! I am so glad you could make it," she declared. "I was a little afraid you might have more important business to attend to."

"Nothing would have kept me away," he said, returning the smile.

Then Mrs. O'Flaherty introduced him to the rest of the residents—Enoch, who was holding Jacob on his lap, Mary Appleton and Polly, and their newest arrival, Alma Hansen.

"Please, stay seated, Mr. Reeve," the professor said to Enoch. "What a handsome son you have. And full of energy, I see. What is his age?"

"Approaching his second birthday, sir," Enoch said.

"I remember when my boy was that age," Professor Raymond said. "I imagine young Jacob keeps you on your toes."

"That he does," Enoch replied with a father's knowing smile.

The professor turned to Mary and said, "Mrs. Appleton, I want to thank you for the splendid supper you prepared last night. The people who come here for their meals are indeed fortunate to have you in charge of their diets."

When the professor was introduced to Polly, he bowed and said, "It is a great pleasure to meet you, Miss Polly." The little girl, her cheeks glowing, smiled shyly.

Coming to Alma, the professor greeted the young woman in her native tongue. Alma was clearly pleased, and a gentle smile warmed her pale face.

Finally, the professor turned back to Zoe and handed her the box he carried.

"It is from our friend Ed," he said. "He told me to tell you that he wanted you to have this before you see him again."

Zoe took the box and untied the string. The professor noticed that her delicate hand trembled just slightly as she undid the simple knot and that she seemed almost afraid to lift the lid. But when she did, her blue eyes widened in delight.

"How kind of Ed," she said as she lifted a charming nosegay bouquet from the box.

Mary offered to get a vase for the flowers. Letting Polly hold the bouquet, Zoe glanced inside the box and saw a small card, which she tucked into her pocket. No one noticed her swift movement, for Vi and Christine had just entered, followed by Mary with a water-filled glass vase.

Vi greeted the professor and introduced him to Christine, the mission's indispensable housekeeper. Mrs. O'Flaherty said the blessing, and soon everyone was enjoying a breakfast of scrambled eggs, country ham, biscuits and toast, and Mary's hot spiced applesauce. The conversation largely focused on the residents' plans for the day. Vi and Mrs. O'Flaherty made a special effort to draw Alma into the talk, and the professor, too, conversed with her in German.

Making an Impression

The meal was just finished when Emily Clayton and Dr. Bowman arrived, followed several minutes later by Seth Fredericks. There was another round of greetings. The nurse and the physician were thrilled to see the professor, whom they had both met during his December visit to India Bay. Mr. Fredericks was especially pleased to meet a fellow academic and teacher, and Vi suggested that the professor might like to join him in the classroom that morning.

"Yes, that would be excellent, if you agree," Mr. Fredericks said to the professor.

"I do, sir," the professor replied with interest.

Any further conversation was cut short by the sounds of children talking and laughing in the front hall.

"My students are arriving," Seth Fredericks said jovially. "Come to the classroom, Professor, and meet my young scholars. Perhaps you might tell them something of your work . I understand that you have seen the excavations at Troy."

Professor Raymond turned questioningly to Vi. Her smile dimpling, Vi said, "I warned you, Professor, that we would put you to work. So the classroom shall be your first assignment."

The professor and Mr. Fredericks excused themselves, and Vi started clearing the table as everyone else hurried off to their duties—all except Zoe, who still sat at the table, gazing at the colorful nosegay.

"I told you that Ed would apologize," Vi said, "though I didn't expect him to do so in such a pretty way."

"It's a message," Zoe said softly, "in the language of flowers. Your brother has often joked about my interest in the code of flowers, so this is doubly thoughtful of him, I think. He must have found a florist who knows the meaning of the symbols."

Violet's Perplexing Puzzles

Vi sat down beside Zoe and asked, "Can you read his message in the blossoms?"

Zoe reached out and gently touched a deep red rose in the center of the bouquet.

"This dark red rose means embarrassment and shame," Zoe said. "The purple iris is a messenger. I suppose he means that the bouquet is a message of apology."

"I see some lilies of the valley," Vi said, examining the nosegay closely.

"Those usually mean a return of happiness," Zoe explained.

"Then Ed must be saying he will be happy again if you accept his apology," Vi commented. Pointing to a small cluster of delicate white flowers, she said, "These are narcissus."

"Yes, and I don't understand them. Narcissus symbolizes egotism," Zoe replied.

Vi smiled and said, "I believe that my brother is apologizing for his pride and temper—for not considering your feelings when he spoke harshly last night."

"Do you think that is it?" Zoe asked hopefully. "I thought it might be his way of telling me that I am too conceited."

"In the first place, Ed doesn't think that," Vi said firmly. "And in the second place, he wants your forgiveness for *his* failings, not the other way around. Oh, look! Around the edges are violets! I know their meaning: faithfulness. I shall never forget the little bouquet of violets you gave me when Grandpapa and I left Rome. Maybe Ed remembered my story of your loving gift to me."

Touching the delicate petals of the rose again, Zoe said, "You knew that Ed would apologize, and he has. But he has

deprived me of my chance to practice being patient. He must have been up before dawn, raiding someone's hothouse for all these spring flowers. I don't know how I could have been so angry with him."

Zoe stood suddenly and grabbed up the flowers in their vase. "I can't moon over these flowers all day," she declared in a lighthearted tone. "I have work to do. I promised to help Alma with the clothing. Anyway, I will take these flowers with me. They're just in the way here."

Zoe hurried off before Vi could respond. And Vi, who knew her friend's moods very well, didn't try to stop her. She began to gather up the last of the breakfast things.

Vi did not see the professor again until almost noon. She worked in her office for a while — taking care of correspondence and selecting the Bible verses she would read for the devotion she led every day after the mission's afternoon meal. Then she went to the storage room where Zoe and Alma were sorting clothing. Zoe was separating the items by sizes, and Alma was already busy with her needle and thread. The three young ladies discussed several issues regarding the best way to distribute the clothing, and Zoe made the very practical suggestion that the mission acquire a sewing machine. Vi had some ideas about how this might be accomplished, and she promised to get to work on it immediately.

Then she went to the kitchen where Mrs. Stephens and another lady from her church were helping Mary and preparing the food baskets that they would deliver to the needy. After consulting with them about several matters, Vi moved on to the meeting room. Mrs. O'Flaherty and Polly were setting the table and discussing their afternoon excursion to the business section of India Bay. Hearing Polly's excited chatter about riding the streetcar, having tea in a restaurant, and visiting the city's new library, Vi had half a mind to join them. But she had more pressing duties.

She proceeded upstairs to the clinic, where she saw the Widow Amos—who invariably visited the clinic on Fridays, when Dr. Bowman was in—sitting on one of the benches that lined the hallway.

Spotting Vi, Mrs. Amos called out in her no-nonsense way, "Did you hear about the fire? Bessie Moran's kitchen went up in flames last night. Some of her boarders put it out before it spread to the house, but Bessie won't be doin' much cooking for a time."

Vi hurried to the older woman and asked anxiously, "Was anyone injured?"

"No more than a few scratches and coughing from the smoke, praise the Lord," Mrs. Amos said. "Kitchen's pretty well gone, and Bessie's little laundry room. Don't know how the fire started, but I wouldn't be surprised if it wasn't that old cook stove of hers. The vent's near rusted away, and it's easy enough for sparks to fly out and catch something. Happened about ten o'clock last night."

"I was up at that time, but I didn't hear any fire engines," Vi said.

"Not that you would," snorted a man sitting next to Widow Amos. Vi had not seen him before, but she saw that he had a heavy bandage around his arm.

The man went on, "Firemen don't want to come into Wildwood. Even if they did, by the time someone could get to 'em to raise the alarm, they'd be too late to do any good.

Making an Impression

We gotta handle things for ourselves here, and what we can't handle just burns to the ground."

"Bessie's all right," Mrs. Amos said. "Don't know what she's gonna do now, though. She offers rooms and meals, but she can't cook without a kitchen. She might lose her lodgers or have to cut her rents. Can't charge for cookin' when you ain't got nothing to cook with."

Vi asked more questions, all the while thinking what could be done to help Miss Moran. Then Dr. Bowman came to get the Widow Amos, and Vi excused herself. She was heading to the back stairs just as Professor Raymond emerged from the classroom, which was located at the rear of the hallway.

"Oh!" Vi cried. "You startled me."

"I'm sorry. It wasn't intentional," the professor said.

"I know," Vi replied with a smile. "My mind was on something else. I've just learned that one of our neighbors had a fire last night, and I must find out what she needs."

"Perhaps I can be of service," the professor offered.

"Well, I'm sure she needs food," Vi said as they descended the narrow staircase. "Miss Moran runs a boardinghouse, and her kitchen was destroyed. She and her boarders will have no food. But Enoch and the ladies of the church have so many other deliveries to make. Mrs. O'Flaherty is taking Polly into the city, and Mary and Zoe have the schoolchildren's lunch to serve. Would you be able to accompany me, Professor Raymond?"

"I would be happy to," he said.

They reached the bottom of the steps and entered the kitchen. Vi quickly told the others what had occurred, and then she remembered to introduce the professor to Mrs. Stephens and her helper. The ladies were just filling the last

Violet's Perplexing Puzzles

of the food baskets, and they began to prepare additional baskets for Miss Moran and her boarders.

"We'll take the buggy," Vi told the professor. "Miss Moran lives only a few blocks from here. It's a short walk, but we have too much to carry."

"Enoch's out in the stable," Christine said. "I'll tell him right now to hitch up the horse." And she rushed out the back door.

Vi hurried down to the cellar, and a few minutes later, she reappeared with a box full of tinned meats and canned vegetables and fruits. The professor took the heavy box from her arms and set it on a counter. Vi was already rummaging through the pantry and packing another box with some cups and bowls, utensils, and several cooking pots. In a third box, she put packages of essentials—flour, salt, sugar, a couple of loaves of bread, and a container of coffee.

"Can we spare two bottles of milk?" she asked Mary.

"We can make do without 'em well enough," Mary replied.

The professor had been watching all of this activity with sharply observant eyes. In truth, he was amazed at the way the women worked together. He wasn't sure what he had expected, but it was not such clear thinking and rational organization. They all seemed to know exactly what needed to be done, and they went to their tasks with a calm, swift efficiency. Fifteen minutes after Vi had told him about the fire, the buggy was standing outside the kitchen, and the professor was helping Enoch load the back with the boxes and baskets. Mrs. Stephens had brought Vi's coat and hat and the professor's overcoat.

"I'll drive," Vi said. "I know the way."

110

Making an Impression

Professor Raymond didn't argue. He climbed into the passenger seat and placed the last of the food baskets at his feet.

The kitchen door swung open, and Mary came out, holding a covered pail and a paper sack. She handed both to the professor.

"That's today's soup and some fresh cornbread," she said. "Now you make Miss Bessie eat. She needs to keep her strength up. Tell her we're all praying for her. And hold down the lid on that pail, or you'll have bean soup all over that nice coat."

"I'll give her your message," he said as Vi cracked the reins, expertly guided the buggy through the mission's gates, and turned onto Wildwood Street. She held the horse at a safe pace as they proceeded along the broken and rutted street. Minutes later, they were knocking at the front door of Miss Moran's boardinghouse.

"What if she is not at home?" the professor asked.

"Then we'll leave the food here, and I'll return later," Vi said.

"Won't all this be stolen if it is left unattended?" he worried.

"That is a possibility, but not likely," Vi replied. She looked up into the professor's face and said with a wry smile, "Gentlemen are not the only people who live by a code of honor, Professor. The people of Wildwood understand suffering, and their inclination is to help their neighbors when they can—especially in times of trouble. I doubt anyone would take advantage of Miss Moran. Her neighbors will want to share what little they have with her. The food we've brought will save them from sacrificing their own—which they would do without regret. That is one of the reasons why I was so anxious to get here quickly. When her neighbors see that we have brought food, they will find other ways to help."

"And no one will go hungry," the professor said thoughtfully.

"That is the goal," Vi said.

She was about to knock once again when the door opened and Miss Bessie Moran peeked out. She was a small, plump, pretty woman of about forty, but today she looked ten years older. Her face was drawn and almost gray in the thin light of the overcast winter day. But a little of her natural color came back into her cheeks when she saw Vi.

"Miss Travilla! Come in!" she exclaimed in a voice that reminded the professor of a small bird. "You've heard of our fire," Miss Moran said, leading them into her small parlor. The smell of smoke was strong in the air, and Vi noticed a pile of wet, filthy clothing on the floor near the fireplace.

"Mrs. Amos told me," Vi said, "and we've brought some food for your boarders. Professor Raymond was kind enough to come with me. He is visiting Samaritan House today to see what we do."

"It's a real pleasure to meet you, sir," Miss Moran said to the professor, who returned her greeting with several words of condolence.

The parlor opened into a dining room, and Vi and the professor took their baskets to the table. Then the professor excused himself and went outside to get the other items from the buggy. It took three trips—the last to get the pail of Mary's bean soup.

When he came in, Miss Moran was telling Vi about the fire. "I thank the Lord for Jimmy Farmer," the little woman said. "He's always been as quiet as a mouse since he came to live here, but last night he nearly shouted the house down when he smelled the smoke. He got the men outside, and they did everything they could, but that kitchen was too far gone. So Jimmy had them wetting down the back of the house, so it wouldn't catch alight. They were so brave, Miss Travilla. I felt just awful this morning when they had to go off to work without breakfast. Mrs. Gregory—she and her husband have rooms on the second floor—had some tea, and we gave them that, but without even a spoonful of sugar or a drop of milk."

At this thought, Miss Moran's face crumpled and tears trickled from her eyes. "I'm not sure what to do," she said in trembling tones. "I don't know how I can rebuild the kitchen. If my boarders leave me…"

"Don't worry about that right now," Vi said soothingly. "You are safe and the house is not damaged. But you need to take care of yourself. Is anyone else in the house?"

"Mrs. Gregory."

"Well, we have lunch for you both," Vi said. "And we can make coffee at the fireplace. Mary Appleton said most emphatically that you must keep your strength up, and I believe that her bean soup is almost as good as yours."

Miss Moran went to summon her lodger, and the professor volunteered to fetch water from the well house. This gave him a chance to see the damage done by the fire, and indeed, Miss Moran's kitchen was now only a smoking pile of rubble. He wondered what the poor woman could do to replace this loss. He determined to discuss the situation with Vi when he had the chance.

They stayed about an hour, for Vi wanted to be certain that Miss Moran ate. By the time the women finished their meal, Miss Moran looked much better, and she and Mrs.

Gregory were even able to laugh about how surprised the male lodgers would be to find supper on the table that night.

"I shall never be able to thank you enough for all this," Miss Moran said as she accompanied Vi and the professor to the door.

"It's what friends do," Vi replied. Then she remembered something.

"The clothes near your fireplace. They belong to your male boarders, don't they?" she asked.

"They do. The men were soaked last night."

"Let me take them," Vi said. "We will launder them and have them back to you tomorrow."

The professor was holding the now empty food baskets, and Vi grabbed one and went back into the house to gather up the soiled clothing.

Miss Moran turned anxious eyes to the professor. "She's already done so much. She mustn't…"

"But she will," the professor said. "I do not know Miss Travilla very well, Miss Moran, but I begin to suspect that she is like a force of nature. Once she determines to do something, no one can stop her."

Vi returned with the basket of clothing. The professor took it, and Vi quickly leaned down and kissed Miss Moran's cheek.

"I will be back tomorrow," Vi said.

"God bless you," Miss Moran responded in a soft whisper.

As she watched Vi and the tall gentleman get into the buggy, Miss Moran said to herself, "Keep her safe, dear Lord. She and her friends are a blessing for us all."

114

Making an Impression

Back at Samaritan House, Vi barely had time to report on Miss Moran's situation before people began to arrive for the afternoon meal. Since Mrs. O'Flaherty and Polly had not yet returned from their excursion, Vi, Zoe, and Mary served the meal, while Christine and Alma took the wet and soot-stained clothing to the laundry room in the cellar.

Vi was explaining to Alma what needed to be done, until Christine said with a laugh, "Miss Alma and I might not speak the same language, but washing is washing. We'll get on fine, Miss Vi."

The professor offered to help with the meal, but Vi suggested that he might want to see the clinic and visit with Dr. Bowman instead.

It was getting dark by the time the last of the day's visitors departed and the residents had an opportunity to sit and talk over the day's activities. Dr. Bowman and Emily usually attended Vi's afternoon devotion and then joined the mission staff for a while, but this day they left early in order to call on Miss Moran. She had a mild heart problem, and the doctor wanted to be certain that the stress of the fire had not been too much for her.

By six o'clock, the tables had been cleared and all but a few dishes washed, dried, and put away for the next day. Vi retreated to the parlor area of the meeting room, where Mrs. O'Flaherty was chatting with Professor Raymond. Vi almost collapsed into an armchair.

"What a day!" she declared good-naturedly. "I'm afraid we have run you off your feet, Professor."

The professor grinned and said, "Mrs. O'Flaherty tells me that today's events were not so unusual. I must say that the work you are all doing here is most impressive."

"Thank you," Vi said simply. She wanted to hear more of Mark Raymond's observations, but she was just too tired for serious conversation. And she realized all of a sudden that she was very hungry. This brought a second realization, and she sat up straight and exclaimed, "Oh, Professor Raymond, we haven't given you a bite to eat since breakfast! Where was my head? Will you join us for supper? It will be plain, but very good."

"Do not worry about me," the professor replied. "I am used to working through my lunch. Much as I would like to stay, Professor Kincaid has invited me to dine with him tonight, so I should get back to my hotel."

Mrs. O'Flaherty stood and said, "I'll ask Enoch to bring the buggy."

The professor hurried to his feet, protesting, "That isn't necessary. I will find a cab."

"Not in Wildwood, you won't, Dr. Raymond," Mrs. O'Flaherty replied firmly. "The cabbies of this city rarely come to Wildwood, for there are few people here who can afford their services. Enoch left the buggy hitched when he brought Polly and me back. He will be happy to take you to the hotel."

Mrs. O'Flaherty strode purposefully from the room, and the professor sat down again.

"Today has been an education for me," he said to Vi. His tone was serious. "When we were at Miss Moran's, I thought of my own life and how little attention I pay to those around me who are in need. You have given me an opportunity to see beyond myself, Miss Travilla, and I appreciate that very much. I should like the chance to learn more about Wildwood and India Bay, and I was hoping that you, Mrs. O'Flaherty, and Miss Love might join me for lunch tomorrow. The Bayview Hotel has a very pleasant dining room."

Vi thought for a few seconds, considering the next day's schedule. Then she said, "That would be very nice, Professor. Yes, we will be delighted to join you. But didn't you just say that you often work through the lunch hour?" she added with a sparkling smile.

"I did," he laughed softly. "When I'm working with my students or concentrating on my research, I often forget about everything else, including food. But I am not always so absentminded. The prospect of entertaining three charming ladies is more than enough to keep my attention engaged. Shall we say one o'clock?"

"That would be perfect," Vi said.

Mrs. O'Flaherty returned to say that the buggy was waiting, and the professor took his leave.

Vi told Mrs. O'Flaherty about the professor's invitation, and Mrs. O was clearly pleased by the prospect.

"It was gracious of him to include Zoe and me," she remarked.

"But why wouldn't he?" Vi asked.

"Indeed, why wouldn't he?" Mrs. O'Flaherty said. "I'm sure he just wants to know more about India Bay."

Vi didn't notice her dear companion's smile. As tired and hungry as she was, Vi felt oddly revitalized. It didn't occur to her that her renewed energy might have some connection to the prospect of seeing Professor Mark Raymond again. Her conscious mind was focused on a new problem — how to get fire service to Wildwood.

CHAPTER 9

Many Questions

*For the LORD gives wisdom
and from his mouth come
knowledge and
understanding.*

PROBERBS 2:6

*A*s it happened, the professor decided to stay several days longer in India Bay than he had originally intended, and Vi saw him on a number of occasions. These contacts were perfectly natural: the professor was still weighing his decision about whether to take the position at India Bay University, and he wanted as much information as he could gather.

Luncheon at the hotel was quite a delightful gathering, though too short in duration, because the ladies had to return to the mission to help with the afternoon meal. There was more time the next day; Professor Raymond was invited to accompany Vi and Zoe on their Sunday journey to Ion. After church services and lunch with the family, the professor had a lengthy conversation with Elsie Travilla and Horace Dinsmore about the advantages and the disadvantages of living in the South. Vi did not participate, for the younger Travillas insisted that she, Zoe, and Ed join them for a carriage ride to Roselands to see their cousins, the Conleys, and their elderly great-grandfather, Horace Dinsmore, Sr. The old gentleman, who was exceedingly frail, was now permanently confined to his bed, and a visit from Vi always seemed to cheer him.

While at Roselands, Vi managed to take Zoe aside for the briefest of chats.

"I know you've thanked Ed for the bouquet. Did he say anything interesting?" Vi asked, unable to restrain her curiosity.

Violet's Perplexing Puzzles

"He apologized in words even nicer than his flowers," Zoe smiled, "and he blushed as red as a beet. I kept my resolution to be patient. I listened instead of talking back."

On returning to Ion, Vi was able to spend only another half hour with her family before driving back to the mission. She would have lingered longer, but her mother wanted her to depart while there was still plenty of daylight. Zoe stayed behind, since she was returning to The Oaks and her studies, so Mark Raymond was the only passenger in Vi's buggy. This was Vi's first opportunity to speak to him in private, and she found herself unsure of how their conversation might proceed.

Would it be appropriate for me to ask about his children? Or where his decision about the university position stands? she wondered as she navigated the buggy down the driveway and onto the country road.

The professor solved her dilemma by speaking first and giving her a brief summary of his conversation with Elsie and Horace, Jr.

"I appreciate your mother and grandfather's frankness," the professor said. "They were very open about the differences between North and South and the difficulties I might encounter here. But I must admit that the prospect of your warmer climate and Southern hospitality is very appealing. When I asked your mother about finding a place to live if I should move, she suggested that Mrs. Lansing might be of help."

Vi, smiling to herself, said, "I will arrange a visit with the Lansings if you like. Mrs. Lansing is the perfect one to offer guidance, for no one knows more about India Bay. And she and Dr. Lansing would be so happy to see you again."

Many Questions

Vi began to point out various sites of interest along the road back to the city, and the professor asked her to describe what the countryside would look like when spring arrived.

"It always seems to me that spring comes very suddenly," Vi said. "One day the fields are brown and bare as they are now, and the next day, they are turning green. If it is an early spring, the daffodils may bloom in late February—well before the first blades of grass. I've often seen them waving their yellow heads in the fields and beside the roads, only to be covered by an unexpected snowfall. Yet they return, year after year, to brave the cold and signal to us that God's promise of renewal is again fulfilled. I think I love spring most of all here. There is a softness as the grass and flowers and bushes bloom and the trees begin to bud."

She took the buggy reins in one hand and moved her other arm in a sweeping gesture toward the east. "Those hills," she said, "separate us from the city and provide some protection from the violent storms that can come in from the sea. Yet our spring storms can be spectacular. Our Papa taught us never to fear the lightning and thunder, for they bring the rain that nurtures every living thing. One of my favorite childhood memories is of being held in my Papa's arms as a thunderstorm rolled in. I must have been about four years old. We were outside, and he was telling me to watch the clouds as they got darker and darker. I remember the wind in my face, and then came raindrops so big that I tried to catch them in my hands. And streaks of lightning that seemed to spread out across the sky like tree branches."

"Weren't you afraid?" the professor asked.

Violet's Perplexing Puzzles

"I probably was," Vi said. "Maybe that's why the memory has stayed with me. But I don't associate it with fear. I remember Papa's arms holding me and how safe I felt. Of course, I know better than to stand outdoors in the height of a storm," Vi added with a laugh. "When I was a little older, Papa made sure I understood the dangers. He taught us to be cautious but not afraid. He always said that fear is the enemy of good sense and wise thinking."

"Your father sounds like a wise man," the professor said. "I wish that I—"

He stopped himself suddenly, and after several moments, Vi dared to venture a remark.

"Perhaps you wish that you had more time with your children," she said.

"Yes, I do," he replied. "But I fear that fatherhood is not so natural with me. I envy you your memories of your Papa. My own died when I was an infant, and I haven't even a picture of him. So I have no model of fatherhood except what I see among the men I know. I have friends, good men all of them, who assure me that a father's duties are to provide materially for their children and apply the necessary discipline. They tell me this is the modern way. I know my friends love their children yet are almost strangers to them. They see their youngsters for a few minutes each morning and each evening, all according to the strictest schedule, and tell themselves that they will be more involved when the children are older."

"I know what you mean," Vi said. "I've heard some people call it 'the children's hour'—that brief time when the little ones are trotted out to greet and kiss their papas and then returned to their nursemaids without complaint. I don't understand it, for my own dear father was so much a part of our daily lives. He and Mamma always said that they were partners in everything, especially in parenthood."

"Your father was fortunate that his work did not take him away from his family," the professor said. "I was so busy with my career that I had little time with my children when they were infants. My dear wife took all the responsibility, and she…"

The professor's voice faltered, and Vi cast a quick glance at him. His expression was distracted, and Vi regretted raising a subject that was so painful for him. She determined to change the mood, so after a minute's silence, she asked, "Are you still planning to go to Mexico in the summer?"

"Um? Mexico?" the professor replied a little uncertainly, almost as if he been awakened in the midst of a dream. Then his voice changed, resonating with strength. "Yes, I will go to Mexico," he said, "in late June. A colleague of mine is mounting an expedition to what he believes is an ancient temple site, and I will join him and his crew for six weeks. It will be training for me in excavating in the jungle."

"I thought your interest was in the Mediterranean region," Vi observed.

"It was, but I have become increasingly curious about past civilizations in our own hemisphere. This will be my first dig in the Americas."

"Dig?" Vi asked.

The professor chuckled and said, "That's how some in my profession are now referring to our work. It's quite apt, for excavation is our chief activity. We dig in the dirt and sift every particle in search of clues as to how people lived hundreds and thousands of years ago. Whatever is found must be recorded and catalogued in exact detail. The popular press makes archaeology sound like a grand and dangerous adventure. But the truth is that the work is slow and tedious and often unrewarding when one doesn't find what one is looking for."

"Yet it must be done if you are to gain the knowledge you seek," Vi said. "I'd like to know more about what you do. How is a dig organized?"

"Well, one must first find the money to pay for the trip and equipment and to hire local workers. That can take longer than an expedition itself. The costs are far beyond the average scholar's capabilities, so one must have generous benefactors. And then…" he paused. "Do you really want to hear about this?" he asked.

"I do," Vi said with interest. She was not merely being nice. She really wanted to know about his occupation. More important, she hoped to better understand this complicated man whom she had once dismissed as dull and arrogant. But since their first meeting, he had shown himself to be capable of great kindness and self-sacrifice, and she could never forget his efforts to solve the mystery of Tansy and Marigold's family. Though the professor tried to hide his private suffering, Vi had seen that as well—at least hints of it whenever he spoke of his three children and his long absences from them. Over the past few days, she had observed another side—the sociable and good-humored professor who seemed to take such pleasure in being with friends. Yet there was also the reticence he had displayed just moments before, when he had almost expressed his feelings but pulled back into himself.

What a complex person you are, Professor Raymond, Vi thought to herself as he began to explain the organization and purpose of an archaeological dig. *You devote yourself to unraveling the puzzle of lives lived in the distant past. At the same time, you are so reluctant to disclose anything about your-self. You haven't even mentioned the letter you sent to me. Do you regret having made even those brief references to your family? Or did I misunderstand your intent? And why am I so curious about you?*

She quickly put aside her questions and listened attentively to what he was saying. The more he told her, the more interested she became. Despite his contention that the work was tedious, it sounded like an adventure to her. His excitement about his work was infectious, and she began to picture what it might be like to travel to distant and exotic locales in search of the past. He was most animated when he described the discoveries that others were making, and Vi realized that he was ambitious to make his own contributions to this new field of study.

"An archaeologist is a kind of pioneer," she said thoughtfully at one point. "You open new territories, don't you? But your territory is knowledge. You explore the past to help us understand the present."

"That is a good way to describe it," the professor said with an appreciative smile. "Young people rarely comprehend the importance of history, yet you seem to, Miss Travilla. I think perhaps you do understand why this kind of work matters so much."

His tone conveyed some of the archness that had so annoyed her when they first met, but this time she didn't even notice.

After leaving the professor at his hotel, Vi drove straight to the mission, where Mrs. O'Flaherty met her at the door.

Violet's Perplexing Puzzles

She inquired if it had been a pleasant day, and Vi told her that it had been particularly nice.

"We went to Roselands," Vi said as she hung up her cloak, "and Aunt Louise asked me to deliver her fond greetings to you. I asked her and Virginia to come to the city someday soon and visit us. And did you have a good day? Any problems?"

"Not really," Mrs. O'Flaherty said with a flatness in her voice that was quite out of character for her.

They went into the meeting room where a cheerful fire and a pot of tea were waiting.

"What does 'not really' mean?" Vi asked as she warmed her hands at the fireplace. "It's not like you to be coy."

Mrs. O poured the tea and handed a cup and saucer to Vi. "If I sound coy, it's because I'm not sure what I am talking about. And you know how I try to avoid leaping to conclusions without any evidence."

Vi moved to the sofa and sat down. "Evidence of what?"

"That was a bad choice of word," Mrs. O'Flaherty said. " 'Evidence' sounds as if a crime had been committed. I merely observed something that seemed as if it might indicate a problem. But it probably isn't a big problem, so I want you to take what I say with a very large grain of salt, Vi girl."

Mrs. O'Flaherty took a drink of tea and then said, "It's our young *fraulein*. As you know, I had asked Alma to attend church with me today, and she had seemed happy at the prospect. But after you and Zoe left this morning, Alma came to my room and told me that she had decided not to go. I was afraid she might not be feeling well; however, she said she was fine. Perhaps it was impolite, but I pressed her for a reason. She tried to avoid my questions. At last, she said that it would 'not be right' for her to go. And that is all I could learn. I've shared my devotions with the girl each night since she came to us, and I know that she is a devout Christian. So I cannot fathom why it would not be right for her to attend church."

"Where is Alma now?" Vi asked.

"In her room. She retired early. And she barely ate a bite of her lunch or supper," Mrs. O'Flaherty said.

"Maybe she is just tired," Vi suggested. "Coming here and then insisting on working almost from the moment she set foot in the mission — that would be a drain on anyone's energies."

"I thought of that," Mrs. O'Flaherty said. "I also considered that she may have hesitated to go to church because of language. It is hard to meet people when you do not speak their language. And she is a shy girl. It could be a combination of all those things. But there is another matter."

"What?" Vi asked. In truth, she was thinking that Mrs. O'Flaherty might be overreacting. Vi remembered with great affection what a devoted guardian Mrs. O had been to her when she was a girl going off on her first adventures — the trip to Lansdale and then the sudden emergency that had taken them to Rome. She thought about their summer in New York City, when she and Mrs. O'Flaherty had been so worried about Zoe (needlessly as it turned out) and when Mrs. O had befriended Louise Conley, despite Louise's rude temper.

Mrs. O'Flaherty laid her cup on the table and said, "When I returned from church, Alma was not here. She came in just as Mary and Polly and I were sitting down to lunch. She said that she had gone for a walk because she wanted some fresh air. But she didn't have the look of someone who had just taken a stroll. A walk in the chill air should have put roses in her cheeks, but her face was even more pale and wan than on that first morning we met her. And she was agitated. As I said, she barely ate anything, and after our Bible discussion, she shut herself in the storeroom, saying she wanted to work on her sewing. When I called her to supper, I thought I saw evidence—oh, that word again—that she had been crying."

To this point, Vi had been curious, but now she was becoming concerned.

"Mr. Clinch told us that she cried a great deal," Vi said, "but I haven't seen signs of tears over the last few days. Quite the opposite. I've frequently seen that shy smile of hers, and several times when I passed the storeroom, I heard Alma and Zoe laughing like schoolgirls. Do you think Alma is sad that Zoe left? They seem to have forged a friendship over the last few days."

"That might be it," Mrs. O'Flaherty mused. "I know the girl misses her homeland and family terribly. Did I tell you that she has a brother somewhere in the United States?"

Vi's velvety brown eyes widened. "A brother? But where—why—?"

"I'm sorry. I thought I told you," Mrs. O'Flaherty said. "Alma first mentioned him the night she came to us. Apparently he emigrated a year before she did, just after their mother died. He was supposed to send for Alma, but she never heard from him. That is why she came on her own. I don't know any more except that his name is Rudy."

Vi sank back on the sofa and said, "That would explain her agitation and tears. She must be thinking and worrying about her brother all the time, Mrs. O."

"I know," Mrs. O'Flaherty agreed. "But it doesn't explain her decision not to attend church. Why would she think it is *not right* for her to worship in the Lord's house? That, together with the change in her aspect after her walk, is what still bothers me. I can't help myself, Vi. I think there may be more to this than we can begin to suspect."

Vi sighed heavily. "Do you think we were mistaken to take her in, Mrs. O? I have made quite a few hasty decisions since we came here. Like hiring Emily and Mary and Mr. Fredericks after only one meeting. Those choices all turned out wonderfully, but I have relied on instinct, and instinct is never flawless."

Mrs. O'Flaherty frowned at Vi. "Don't you go mistrusting yourself, Vi girl," she said sternly. "I certainly do not think it was a mistake to invite Alma to join our household. I have no doubt that she is a good person. I'm only saying that what she needs from us may be more than shelter and employment. Something is going on beneath that shy surface of hers, and we won't be able to help until we know what it is."

"How complex everything is," Vi said with another sigh. "I didn't expect our mission here to be easy, but neither did I expect people to be so very, very complicated. I sometimes wonder how I dare to think I can solve other people's difficulties when I can barely manage my own."

"Why, Violet Travilla!" Mrs. O'Flaherty exclaimed. "You have done a magnificent job of organizing Samaritan House! You've taken on challenges that would send most young ladies running back to their mothers in tears. The mission is already affecting the lives of so many people, and that is due primarily to your courage and your insight. Perhaps I should tell you more often how much I admire your strength of character and your determination to serve others."

Violet's Perplexing Puzzles

Vi laid her hand over Mrs. O'Flaherty's and said, "Thank you, but our accomplishments so far belong to all of us. You and our friends here—each of you is a gift from God to the mission. On my own, I could have done nothing."

"That's true," Mrs. O'Flaherty replied. "But it was you who assembled us. It is your leadership and your steadfast belief in the power of people to help one another that inspire us all."

"You're flattering me," Vi said with a small smile.

"Well, of course I am," Mrs. O'Flaherty agreed. "Everyone needs a dose of sincere flattery on occasion. Compliments that are deserved are a form of incentive. They lift our spirits and encourage us to strive to do even better."

Mrs. O'Flaherty shifted her position on the sofa so she could look into Vi's face and said, "Now tell me about Professor Raymond."

Her request was such an abrupt shift in subject that it caught Vi off guard. "I've never met anyone quite like him," Vi answered without thinking.

Mrs. O'Flaherty's expression remained serious. "Is he one of those personal difficulties you spoke of before? Could it be that the professor is the reason you seem to be questioning your instincts?"

"No!" Vi declared almost harshly. A bright flush flooded her cheeks, and she dropped her gaze to the floor. After several seconds, she said in a softer tone, "Maybe he is. I tried to raise the subject of his family today, and he seemed on the point of telling me his feelings, but then he stopped. He just seemed to shut down. So we spent the ride back to the city talking mostly about his work."

Vi raised her eyes to Mrs. O'Flaherty's and went on in a livelier tone, "What he does is truly remarkable. He tries

to make it sound perfectly ordinary, but when he talks about the digs—that's what archaeologists call their excavations—he just lights up, and that funny smile of his makes me want to laugh, because he so clearly loves his work. I wonder why I ever thought archaeology would be dull. It is fascinating, Mrs. O—just as Rosemary has always said."

Mrs. O'Flaherty allowed herself a smile as she said, "I believe that your little sister's use of the word 'fascinating' refers to the man himself rather than his profession."

Vi blushed again, and she sat forward—reaching out to lift the lid off the teapot as if to check its contents.

"I would say the man is puzzling," Vi said slowly. "He was telling me about some of the artifacts that he saw in Greece and Turkey. He said that most people are disappointed because they expect great treasures, like the gold items found at Troy, but these artifacts are often no more than broken pottery and metal utensils whose purpose isn't always clear and simple pieces of jewelry. Yet to the archaeologist, these things are the real treasure, for they offer a glimpse, just a glimpse, into the everyday lives of people who lived thousands of years ago. It is the mystery of those ordinary lives that intrigues the professor—not the prospect of gold or glory. He said that an archaeologist could spend a lifetime studying the remnants of a civilization and still not unravel the secrets of its people. But that's what draws him to the work. Whatever he learns will be passed on to others, and they will continue the study and perhaps find answers."

Vi set the lid back on the teapot and picked up a teaspoon that rested on the table. She turned it over, examining it closely.

"I wonder what this teaspoon would mean to an archaeologist in the future," she said. "What might it reveal about our lives today?"

"I think you may have learned a good deal more about Professor Raymond today than you realize," Mrs. O'Flaherty commented.

Vi turned to look at her, asking, "How do you mean?"

"Only that he is, perhaps, like those pieces of ancient pottery or metal," Mrs. O'Flaherty replied. "The man who seemed so pompous at first has still not revealed himself. Today, you saw his passion for his work. You also saw again his reluctance to discuss his family. At the same time, dear girl, I think that he is reaching out to you for help. The letter that he sent you—those were not the words of a man who is deliberately trying to hide his secrets. No more than a piece of pottery intends to mask its purpose or deceive the archaeologist. It is possible that he is searching for a unique friend who has the patience to help him lift the burden from his heart."

"But he has friends," Vi protested. "Very good friends. I know Ed would do anything he could for Professor Raymond."

"Indeed he would," said Mrs. O'Flaherty. She stood up and began to collect the tea things, putting them onto a tray.

"It's just possible the professor knows that Ed is currently too preoccupied with his own problems of the heart to be of much help to anyone else," Mrs. O'Flaherty said knowingly. "But I also think that the professor has other reasons for reaching out to you, my dear girl."

"Whatever do you mean, Mrs. O?" Vi asked.

"That is part of the puzzle," the older woman replied. "He has shared a lot of his feelings with you, but it comes in bits

and pieces. It will take time and patience to put the pieces together. The question is whether you want to take the time. It is not as if he is the only person who needs your help. It's up to you to decide if you really want to solve the puzzle of Professor Raymond. Perhaps you should look into your own heart, my dear, before you make that decision."

Vi had no response, for Mrs. O's final statements had hit too close to the mark. Could she be that "unique friend" Mrs. O'Flaherty had spoken of? Did she have the patience? She didn't know the answer, but she knew who did. She must talk to the Lord and seek His guidance. It was no longer enough for her just to include the professor in her prayers, she realized. She had to turn to her Heavenly Friend and ask Him to help her understand her own feelings.

Vi hurried into the kitchen to assist Mrs. O with the last of the tidying up. They talked a little more of Alma, deciding that their best course of action was to keep a close watch on the young woman as she settled in, but not to confront her directly. Mrs. O'Flaherty decided to ask Alma to join her for Polly's lessons, and they could work on improving Alma's English. It would also be good for Polly to be exposed to a foreign language.

Nothing more was said about the professor, but Vi's mind was full of him. She looked at her watch and saw that it was just a few minutes after seven o'clock—almost an hour before the Reeves would join the residents of the house for their Sunday evening devotion. Telling Mrs. O'Flaherty that she had a few things to attend to, Vi excused herself and went to her office. She lit the oil lamp on her desk, which shed a soft but thin light about the room. Vi then sat in the desk chair, took a deep breath, closed her eyes, and opened her heart to her Lord and Savior.

She never planned what she would say; she simply let her words and thoughts flow, knowing that the Lord understood their meaning even if she did not. She confessed to Him her sense of being inadequate to meet all the challenges of the mission and her sense that she might be too trusting—and too naïve—to counsel others. She told Him about Alma and her concerns for this lonely girl. She told Him about her worries for the professor. Did he really need her help, or was she misreading everything he said to her? And then she asked for His blessings on everyone she loved, making a special plea for Ed and Zoe—that they might resolve their differences and be granted the happiness that each of them deserved.

She felt much better when she ended her prayer. She had no specific answers to her questions, but this, like all her conversations with the Lord, had brought consolation, encouragement, and relief for her weariness. As long as she loved Him, she knew, she would never feel hopeless or helpless. As long as she put her hope in Him, He would guide her steps, as Psalm 25 often reminded her: "Guide me in your truth and teach me, for you are God my Savior, and my hope is in you all day long."

CHAPTER

10

A Storm of the Heart

*Many waters cannot quench
love; rivers cannot wash
it away.*

Song of Songs 8:7

A Storm of the Heart

*T*here was no decrease in activity at Samaritan House as a new week began. On Monday morning, Vi realized that she'd forgotten to turn her desk calendar to February, but she did remember to contact Mrs. Lansing. That efficient lady responded immediately, inviting her young friend and the professor to come to tea the next afternoon.

So Tuesday afternoon saw Vi hurrying her horse and buggy through the city streets. *It's a good thing I didn't offer to get the professor at his hotel, or he'd be late as well,* she thought as she maneuvered her vehicle through the busy traffic. There'd been a minor problem just before she left the mission; her business ledger was missing and searching for it delayed her departure for the Lansings'. The crowds on India Bay's main thoroughfare slowed her progress even more. She was flushed with frustration when she at last entered the Lansings' house to find not only her hostess and the professor, but also Dr. Lansing and Dr. Bowman waiting in the parlor.

Her apologies were instantly accepted, and without dwelling on the matter, Vi took a seat. She was determined not to let her own breach of manners, which was not deliberate, interfere with this rare break from her normal weekday routine.

Presiding over a large tea set and a delicious spread of sandwiches and delicate pastries, Mrs. Lansing had been extolling the virtues of India Bay to her guests. Learning that Professor Raymond had three children (and logically assuming that they would accompany him if he made the move South), she assured him that he would find a number of charming neighborhoods where families with children were in the majority. When she asked what type of house he might be looking for, the professor admitted that he really didn't know. So Mrs. Lansing suggested that he meet with a real estate agent. The good lady said, "It could not hurt to learn about the domestic accommodations available here. I have worked with this agent before, and he's a trustworthy businessman. Would tomorrow morning be convenient, if he is free?"

When the professor agreed, Mrs. Lansing excused herself and left the room. In a matter of minutes, she returned, saying, "It's all arranged, Professor Raymond. The agent will come to your hotel at ten o'clock tomorrow morning."

Dr. Lansing noticed the astonished look on Vi's face and said to her in a gleeful tone, "You are wondering how my efficient wife organized the meeting so quickly. It's because of our newfangled invention! We are now on the telephone line, Violet, and it's most phenomenal. Imagine, someone at the hospital can contact me in just moments when I am needed there. It's expensive to have a telephone, but if this invention catches on, I believe we will see the day when they are as essential to every home as gaslights."

Vi asked several questions about the telephone service; then the conversation turned to India Bay University. Since Dr. Lansing had been on the faculty of the University's medical college for many years and Dr. Bowman had earned his degree there, they were able to give the professor valuable insights into what he could expect if he joined the faculty.

Vi made the effort to listen, but her thoughts drifted back to the subject of the telephone. Her mind churned with ideas. If there were telephones in Wildwood, would that not improve life for everyone? To be able to telephone the fire station or the police or the hospital and summon help in an emergency!

The men were deep in a discussion about "University politics," so Vi turned to Mrs. Lansing, and in a soft voice, she asked, "Might I see your telephone?"

"Of course you may," Mrs. Lansing replied. "It's not a pretty thing. But I can demonstrate how it works, if you like."

Telling the men to continue their conversation, Mrs. Lansing led Vi to the back hallway and pointed to an odd wooden box that hung on the wall. In her brisk fashion, she showed Vi the listening and speaking devices and explained how operators connected calls.

"Just don't ask me to tell you how the voices travel from one location to another," Mrs. Lansing chuckled. "It's all done along wires, I'm told, like the telegraph. But to me, it is more of a magician's trick. I see it, I believe what I see, but I have no idea how it is done."

Vi was studying the box closely. "However it is done, it would be a blessing if we could have a telephone in Wildwood," she said. Then she expressed her ideas about a telephone linking the people of Wildwood to the services they needed—the fire fighters, the police, and ambulances.

Mrs. Lansing's brow furrowed with concentration. After some moments, she said, "To have a telephone could literally be a rescue line for Wildwood, but I think it will be some time before it happens. The new telephone companies must make money to stay in business, but there is no one in Wildwood who could afford the service. I don't see how…"

Seeing the look of disappointed resignation on Vi's face, Mrs. Lansing said in a cheery tone, "But we can make inquiries. One should never assume that something is impossible. Would you allow me to take this on as a project? This is just the kind of challenge I relish, my dear."

Vi gladly agreed, for she knew what Mrs. Lansing could accomplish when she was challenged.

As they went back to the parlor, Mrs. Lansing remarked, "I like Professor Raymond a good deal, and I think he would like India Bay. He already has friends here, and that should be an added attraction."

"It might make the move easier," Vi said. "But I believe that the professor has a great many things to consider."

She almost said something about the professor's children and the difficulty of uprooting them from the home of their aunt in Boston. But she held her tongue. She had no right to discuss a matter that, she knew, was painful for Mark Raymond.

"When must he give his decision to the University?" Mrs. Lansing asked.

"I don't know," Vi replied.

"Well, it must be soon, for if he does not take their offer, the University officials will need sufficient time to find other suitable candidates to replace the admirable Professor Kincaid."

Vi hadn't thought of this before. Mark Raymond would have to make his decision soon. Her stomach suddenly felt as if it were twisted in a knot. *What will he do? What if he decides not to come to India Bay? And why does his decision matter so very much?*

⁓

The three visitors left the Lansings' at just a little before six o'clock. Vi's horse and buggy were standing in the driveway, but she lingered to chat while the stableman brought the Lansings' carriage around for the gentlemen. Saying how much he would like to continue their earlier conversations, the professor invited Vi and Dr. Bowman to join him for dinner at the Bayview Hotel. The doctor accepted eagerly, but Vi had to decline. Mr. Archibald, the carpenter who had supervised so much of the renovation of Samaritan House, was coming to the mission to see her that evening.

So she bade farewell to the gentleman, and Professor Raymond helped her into her buggy.

"I have changed my plans and must leave India Bay in two days," he said as he gathered the buggy reins for her. "I need to speak with you. May I call on you before I go?"

"Oh, yes, please do," Vi said, hoping that her voice didn't betray her emotions. The news of his sudden departure literally shook her, and she struggled to keep her voice steady and light as she continued, "Everyone at the mission would like to see you again before you go. Come tomorrow, after you have seen the real estate agent."

The night was dark, but the house lights illuminated his face, and Vi could see a strange expression come over the professor's countenance. His smile faded, and his eyes seemed riveted on hers. He gave her the reins, and then he clasped her gloved hands tightly in both of his.

"Tomorrow will—" he said, breaking off suddenly. His voice had been oddly deep and urgent, and Vi knew there was more he wanted to say.

He stared at Vi a second or two longer. Then he dropped his hold on her hands, backed away a step, and bowed slightly. In his normal resonant baritone, he resumed, "Tomorrow will be splendid, Miss Travilla. I look forward to visiting Samaritan House once more."

Violet's Perplexing Puzzles

Vi could not make herself speak. She managed a nod at the professor, and she drove off in a state of utter bewilderment. She told herself that she had just imagined the look in his eyes and the tone of his voice. But he had taken her hands. She could still feel the strength of his grip. That had been *real*. Without being able to explain it, she knew that his look, tone, and touch were meant as a message. In those few moments, he had dropped all his barriers. The real Mark Raymond had stood before her and gripped her hands. A phrase that Mrs. Lansing had used flashed into her head—"rescue line." For the briefest of instants, Mark had held her hands as if she were the only person in the world who could pull him to safety.

Vi was barely conscious of what she was doing as the buggy clattered over the cobblestone streets toward the rough road of Wildwood. She kept replaying those moments in her mind, and her heart. The look, the touch, the sound of his voice. She struggled to make sense of them.

Then she remembered what he'd said, that he was leaving in two days. *Why? Has he already made his decision? Has he decided not to return to India Bay? Is that what he will tell me tomorrow?* The thought sent a chill of fear through her, and there were tears on her cheeks when she turned into the gates of Samaritan House.

As she reined the horse to a slow walk, she spoke softly into the cold night air. "What do you want to tell me? Two more days, and you will be gone. And then what shall I do? What shall I do without you?"

Without realizing it, she had dropped the reins, and the horse made his own way around the house and to the stable. He twisted his head, flipping his mane, and stood still—waiting for someone to come and unhitch him as always.

Vi simply sat in the buggy, as if she were also awaiting someone to come forward and take control. A prayer formed in her mind: *Please, dear Lord, lead me onto Your path. I don't understand what has happened, and I need You to show me the way out of my confusion. Show me which way to turn. I want to be strong, but I feel so weak and uncertain. I need You, Lord, to help me. I need You to light my path…and Mark's.*

The sound of a voice interrupted her desperate pleas, and Vi turned to see Enoch approaching from the carriage house. He was holding a lamp, and the familiar sight of his tall figure brought a wave of relief to her. She was home now, among her Samaritan family. Here was shelter and understanding. Her Heavenly Father had answered her prayer. He had guided her home and reminded her where her own hope lay—in Him above all and in the hearts of the wonderful people who were awaiting her return.

"Mr. Archibald's inside to see you," Enoch was saying. "He seems all excited about his plans for that elevator. I'll unhitch old Robin and give him his supper. You go on inside now."

"Thank you," Vi said, coming back to herself. She hurriedly wiped at her cheeks, and then she stepped down from the buggy.

"Did anything happen while I was away?" she asked.

"Were you expecting something out of the ordinary to happen today, Miss Vi?" Enoch answered with a laugh.

"No, no," Vi said as she turned toward the house. "I wasn't expecting anything unusual at all."

By sheer willpower, Vi forced herself to put Mark Raymond from her mind when she greeted Mr. Archibald.

Violet's Perplexing Puzzles

For the next hour, she and the master carpenter reviewed his detailed plans for the construction of the elevator, which would transport disabled patients to the clinic. Vi promised to consult with her brother and with Dr. Bowman and Miss Clayton as quickly as possible, and she expressed her hope that construction could begin as soon as the weather allowed. Entrusting his drawings to her, Mr. Archibald left Samaritan House a happy man.

Vi joined Mrs. O'Flaherty, Alma, Mary, and Polly in the kitchen for supper.

Mrs. O'Flaherty noticed that Vi seemed quieter than usual, but she attributed her young friend's mood to the fatigue of a busy social afternoon. Mrs. O felt no concern when Vi said that she was tired and went to her room immediately after they had washed and put away the dishes.

In truth, Vi was anxious to be alone so that she might search for some solution to her confusion. Most nights, she selected one sacred passage to read and meditate on before her bedtime. Tonight, however, she scurried like a mouse through the pages of her well-worn black Bible, searching out one passage after another and weaving their messages into a whole. Several times she came back to the Gospel of Luke and the story of Jesus and His disciples in the storm. Jesus had suggested that they sail to the opposite side of the lake, but while He slept in the boat, a storm came up and threatened to sink their vessel. "The disciples went and woke him, saying, 'Master, Master, we're going to drown!' He got up and rebuked the wind and the raging waters; the storm subsided, and all was calm. 'Where is your faith?' he asked his disciples. In fear and amazement they asked one another, 'Who is this? He commands even the winds and the water, and they obey him.'"

146

Having read these verses one last time, Vi closed the book and put it aside. She pictured herself as a passenger in the boat. She imagined her own fear and that of all the other passengers as the waves crashed over the sides. In her mind's eye, she envisioned sails shredding like paper as the wind lashed at them. She could almost feel the cold water that poured into the boat and lapped at her feet. From a place deep in her memory, she recalled the time when she and her family had been at risk in a raging sea, and that brought back the sounds of the howling storm and people crying out in their fear.

Then she imagined Jesus standing and boldly commanding the winds to cease and the waters to retreat. And there in her room, she felt an indescribable sense of peace wash over her. For a long time, she sat and basked in the full knowledge of His saving grace. She needed only to put herself in His hands, and He would protect her and lead her to the right choices. She had been feeling something like panic ever since Mark had told her of his departure and then grasped her hands, but now it slipped away. Her mind cleared, and she began to put her reason to work.

If I am to help Professor Raymond and myself, I must first be honest with myself about my own feelings, she told herself. *What do I feel? Is Mark just a friend or does he hold a special place in my heart?*

She rose from her seat on her bed and went to her dressing table. She stared at herself in the mirror and said to her reflection, "Violet Travilla, it's time to admit the truth to yourself. You love Mark Raymond. There! You've said it. You are in love."

She leaned closer to the mirror so that she could see little more than her own eyes.

"You don't know if he could love you in return, but that isn't the issue," she went on, her voice growing steadier. "Mark is in trouble and pain. In his way, he has reached out to you. Are you going to turn him away just because you are afraid he may not feel the same affection for you that you feel for him? Do your own feelings make you any less of a friend?"

She turned from the mirror, and her gaze traveled around her room—stopping on a painting that hung on the wall over her bed. It was the work of her brother-in-law, Lester Leland. From her own sketches, he had created a scene in a sunlit Roman market square and filled it with portraits of the family members and friends who were so important to her that summer four years ago.

A little smile came to her lips as she thought, *There is your answer, in the faces of people who helped you and whom you helped as best you could. No one knew then what the future would bring. We lived in the moment, put our hope in God, and focused on the crisis at hand. We trusted God absolutely. Remember that experience. Whatever the future may hold, it is not yours to control. It is the present that matters. This love you feel may grow, or it may wither away. But whatever happens, Mark needs a friend right now—a true friend who will stand by him and be faithful no matter what. Can you be that friend? Can you put his feelings and his needs above your own?*

A verse from 1 Corinthians 13 came to her mind: "And now these three remain: faith, hope and love. But the greatest of these is love."

She looked again at all the faces in the painting, and her sense of resolve deepened.

"Dear Lord," she prayed aloud, "I know that You are with me, guiding me to be the kind of friend who walks in faith, hope, and love, just as Christ did. I can always share what is in my heart with You. Your love and comfort are my greatest consolation. I won't be afraid of my feelings. I won't be afraid of the storm, because You are with me always. I don't know what tomorrow will bring, but I don't fear it anymore."

CHAPTER

11

Something Amiss

*Does she not light a lamp,
sweep the house and search
carefully until she
finds it?*

LUKE 15:8

Something Amiss

Vi awoke the next morning with a sense of renewal. She had opened her heart, and the Lord had calmed her fears and strengthened her hope. Even before she'd lifted her head from her pillow, she offered a prayer of gratitude to her loving Heavenly Father.

She didn't expect Mark Raymond to arrive until afternoon, and she determined not to let anticipation of his visit distract her from her responsibilities. She rose and dressed quickly; then she turned to her morning devotion—a Bible reading followed by another prayer. She was making her bed—and thinking how hungry she was—when there was a knock at her door.

"Come in," she called out cheerfully.

Mrs. O'Flaherty walked in and said, "Well, from the sound of your voice, I'd say you had a good night's rest."

"I did," Vi replied, "and now I'm ready for a big breakfast and a day of work."

She gave her pillows a final pat and turned the coverlet over them while she talked with Mrs. O'Flaherty.

"Professor Raymond will be coming to the mission today," Vi said. "He is leaving India Bay ahead of schedule, and he wants to see everyone before going."

"Does this mean he has made his decision?" Mrs. O'Flaherty asked.

"I don't know," Vi said. "I suppose he'll tell us if he has. But we have other things to worry about."

She looped her arm into Mrs. O'Flaherty's, and they left the room together.

"Did anyone happen to find my ledger book?" Vi asked. "I searched high and low yesterday, but it was nowhere to be seen."

"I also looked in all the logical places after you left for tea with Mrs. Lansing," said Mrs. O'Flaherty. "I even checked the cellar, thinking you might have put it down when you were doing your inventory of our supplies the other day, but I didn't find it. My husband used to say that the best way to find a thing is to stop looking for it. I'm sure the ledger will turn up where we least expect it."

"Oh, well, it has little value to anyone else," Vi said. "I don't imagine that too many people would find my financial lists to make exciting reading. If it is really lost, Ed will give me one of his serious lectures about the importance of tending to business, but I can reconstruct most of the ledger entries without too much trouble. I keep all my receipts in files, just as Ed has instructed."

They entered the kitchen to find Mary and Christine cooking breakfast. Polly and little Jacob were sitting on the floor in a corner and playing with some blocks. The aroma of coffee brewing and bread toasting reminded Vi again of how hungry she was.

Vi offered to set the big kitchen table, and as she was counting the plates to be sure there were enough for everyone, she noticed that their newest resident was absent.

"Where is Alma?" she asked. "Has she overslept?"

"She went out for a little walk," Christine said. "From what I could make out, she said she'd be back in time for her lessons with Mrs. O and Polly. I think I'm getting to understand a little more of what she says. I just wish I could help her with her sadness."

"Sadness?" Vi questioned.

Something Amiss

Christine motioned Vi and Mrs. O'Flaherty aside and spoke softly so the children couldn't hear: "Alma's a good girl, Miss Vi, but there's something troubling her. I can see it in her eyes. There's a word for that kind of sadness — 'melancholy.' It's a kind of thoughtful sadness that's always with her, even when she seems happy enough."

At that moment, Enoch came in the back door, shutting it quickly to keep out the cold. "It's gonna be a pretty day," he said as they all gathered at the table and he took Jacob on his lap. "The sky's clear, and the sun's shining. I think it might warm toward lunchtime."

"The good Lord's reminding us that spring is coming soon enough," said Mary. She placed a large platter of eggs and sausage on the table. "It's a good day to be thankful to Him for all His blessings."

Vi didn't have time to go to her office after breakfast. Mr. Fredericks arrived early to speak to her about purchasing a map for his classroom.

"Even the little ones are becoming interested in our study of geography," he said with a pleased grin. "I think a large map will help them understand the vastness of our world and our own position relative to other countries and peoples."

Vi agreed to the purchase immediately, and Mr. Fredericks said, "I'll bring you the receipt tomorrow," as he bounded up the stairway toward his classroom.

His mention of a receipt reminded Vi of her missing ledger. She was about to renew her search for it when Emily Clayton came in, and the ledger was again forgotten.

Violet's Perplexing Puzzles

Vi wanted to show Emily the drawings that Mr. Archibald had made, and the two young women went to the clinic to discuss the plans.

A little while later, Vi peeked into the nursery where Mrs. O'Flaherty and Polly were busy with morning lessons. Vi was glad to see Alma with them.

"*Guten Morgen*," Vi said.

"That's 'good morning' in German," Polly declared with a hint of pride. "Miss Alma taught me that."

Hearing her name, Alma smiled at Polly, and then she returned Vi's greeting.

"Did you enjoy your walk?" Vi asked in Alma's language. "Enoch says it will be a lovely day."

Alma lowered her eyes at Vi's question and kept them down as she replied in German, "It was a pleasant walk, and I too think it will be a nice day."

"I've asked Alma to go with me later to the dry goods store," Mrs. O'Flaherty said, also speaking in German. "They should know that she will be making purchases of materials and sewing notions and will be using the mission's account from now on."

"That's a good idea," Vi agreed. Then to Alma she said, "I have some news. When I was at Ion on Sunday, I mentioned to my mother that we hoped to acquire a sewing machine. She has a very good machine that is no longer used much, and she will have it sent to us before the end of the week."

Alma had looked up again as Vi talked, and her face seemed to brighten.

Vi added another bit of news that she believed would cheer the young seamstress: "Zoe spoke so highly of your work that Mamma wonders if you might be interested in doing some dressmaking. My sister Rosemary is thirteen, and she needs two or three spring outfits that look more mature. Would you have time to help her?"

Vi's question brought a real smile to Alma's face. "*Yaa*, Miss Violet," she said. "Thank you very much. I will enjoy making dresses for your sister."

"Then I shall write Mamma today, and perhaps she and Rosemary can visit us next week."

Vi started to leave, but then she remembered something. "Oh, Alma," she said, "whenever you make purchases for the mission, would you please get a sales receipt for me? I have to keep track of every penny we spend here. It's my least favorite task, but it must be done." With a wry smile, she added, "My brother requires good bookkeeping, so I have to save every sales slip."

The smile vanished from Alma's face, and she ducked her head again. "I will, Miss Violet," she responded in a tone so soft that Vi almost couldn't hear the words.

Once in the hallway, Vi paused to ponder the sudden change in Alma's mood. But her ruminations were interrupted when she saw Christine coming toward her—little Jacob bouncing on her hip. Christine was grinning and waving something.

"It's from Pennsylvania!" Christine called out.

Vi hurried forward and took a letter from Christine's outstretched hand. She immediately tore open the envelope.

"It's from Crystal," she said, shuffling through the papers. "And here, there's also a note from Tansy. Let's read that first." Then Vi noticed the curious looks of the people who were now waiting outside the clinic door.

"Let's go to the kitchen so we don't disturb Emily's patients," she said, and she and Christine quickly retreated down the back stairs.

Violet's Perplexing Puzzles

Mary, Mrs. Stephens, and a lady from Mrs. Stephens's church were at work preparing the food baskets for the neighborhood shut-ins. They all greeted Vi, and since she didn't think there was likely to be anything confidential in Tansy's letter, Vi decided to read it aloud. In her excellent script, Tansy had written:

Dear Miss Vi, Mrs. O, and all our friends at Samaritan House,

Marigold and I are having a wonderful time. Our grandparents and our Aunt Idanell are so loving and kind. Grandpa Oscar and Grandma Ethel tell us stories about our Daddy when he was a boy. They have a picture of Mommy and Daddy when they got married, and Marigold and I look at it all the time. It should make us sad, but it doesn't, because our parents look so happy. Auntie Idanell is also very good to us and tells us stories. She is a very good cook, and she bakes cookies every day. We want to help her, but she says that she likes to cook for us. Her husband died a long time ago, and she never had any children of her own.

Our family likes having us here, but we don't think we could live with them. Grandpa Oscar lies in his bed most of the time and takes lots of medicine. Our Grandma and Auntie have to care for him and also do their sewing work. I asked Auntie Idanell if we could stay and help her, but she thinks it might be better if we come for visits. I remember what you said, Miss Violet. You said we would always have a home at Samaritan House. I guess that would be best for us, if it's still all right with you.

Marigold sends her love to everybody. She is having a very good time, but she misses Polly a lot. We both miss all of you very much. We hope it is not too cold there.

From your friend,
Tansy Evans

The last line on the page made Vi smile gently. Below Tansy's careful handwriting was another line in large block letters:

WE MISS JAM TOO. LOVE, MARIGOLD

"What a charming letter," Mrs. Stephens said. "And so well written."

"I don't believe I know these children," said Mrs. Lamar, the church member helping Mrs. Stephens. "Do they attend the mission school?"

Mrs. Stephens and Mary began telling Mrs. Lamar about the two young girls who had been lost in India Bay and were rescued by Vi and Mrs. O'Flaherty. Mrs. Lamar was soon wide-eyed as the story of the girls' adventures unfolded.

Meanwhile, Vi and Christine were sitting at the kitchen table and reading Crystal's letter in silence. When they finished, they knew much more about the condition of the elder Evanses, who were both in very poor health, and why it would not be possible for the girls to remain with their family in Pennsylvania. They also knew the date that Crystal, Ben, and the children would return to India Bay.

"There are some big decisions to make when they all get back," Christine said to Vi.

Violet's Perplexing Puzzles

"It won't be long now," Vi replied. "Another ten days. I shall be overjoyed to see our girls. Reading Tansy's letter is almost like hearing her voice—so sweet and proper and loving."

"Ten days gives you some time for making plans," Christine said in her practical way.

"I know," Vi said with a little sigh. "Decisions have to be made, and there's no longer any reason for delay."

Handing the letter to Christine, she said, "Enoch should read this too. Then we can sit down with Mrs. O and discuss our choices."

"Enoch's getting the cart ready to make the food deliveries," Christine said. "I'll show him the letters now. Then you can share them with Mrs. O'Flaherty and Polly. Polly's gonna be mighty glad to know that her friends are coming home."

Christine stood up, putting the envelope into her pocket. Then she scooped up Jacob, who had been playing under the table. "It's almost time for your nap, little man," she gently told her son. "Let's go see your daddy, so he can kiss you before you sleep."

Jacob's eyelids fluttered at the mention of a nap, but he had sufficient energy to say "Jacob kiss Daddy" over and over as Christine got him into his coat and cap.

Vi saw that Mary and the ladies of the church had their duties well under control. Since her help wasn't needed in the kitchen, she decided to attend to another chore.

"Has anyone seen Jam?" she asked.

"The little cat?" asked Mrs. Stephens.

At Vi's nod, Mrs. Lamar laughed and said, "An orange cat skittered round my feet and flew through that door over there"—she pointed toward the office—"a while ago. Just before you came in, Miss Travilla."

Something Amiss

"Then she's on the window ledge," Vi said with an amused smile. "Thank you, Mrs. Lamar."

⁓

Vi entered her office for the first time that day, closing the door to shut out the sounds from the kitchen. As she expected, Jam was curled up on the window sill. Vi walked over to scratch the cat's head and was rewarded with a low, appreciative purr.

"Marigold wants me to tell you that she misses you very much," Vi said to the cat. "You'll be glad to hear that the girls will be home in ten days, and I'm sure they will be ready to spoil you terribly."

In spite of her resolution to keep her mind on mission business, Vi's thoughts went to Mark Raymond and his children, *Max, Lulu, and Gracie. What are they like,* she wondered. *What are their interests? What do they look like? Do they resemble their father?* (She hoped so.) *And how will they react if their father moves with them to India Bay?*

As she considered the young Raymonds, she glanced over her desk. She saw her eyeglasses just where she'd left them the day before. She thought about all the reading she'd done since then—Mr. Archibald's plans, at least an hour with her Bible last night and more before breakfast, even the letters from Crystal and the girls—and she chided herself for her forgetfulness.

The desk itself was a mess, with papers, files, and magazines scattered about during yesterday's search for her record book. She began sorting the papers. Lifting a file marked "groceries," she saw underneath it—the ledger!

Violet's Perplexing Puzzles

Staring at the familiar gray book, she thought, *Where did that come from? It wasn't here yesterday. I know it wasn't. I went through everything on the desk, and it wasn't here. Could I have become so preoccupied that I simply didn't see it?*

She picked up the book and quickly thumbed through its pages. Nothing seemed out of place. Even the little notes that she had pinned to several pages were undisturbed. Still holding the ledger, she slumped back in her chair and closed her eyes, pinching the bridge of her nose as she tried to figure out how she had missed the obvious.

Maybe I am trying to handle too much, she thought. *I forget my spectacles. I think I've lost my ledger when it is right here in front of me. And I keep forgetting to tell people important things. I should have mentioned the sewing machine to Alma when I returned from Ion on Sunday, but I forgot until today. I've always been a well-organized person, but I seem to be spinning lately—making myself giddy with details. Despite what Mrs. O said, I begin to doubt my ability to manage all that I've taken on. Dr. Frazier warned me not to try to do everything. She said it many times, that serving others requires common sense. She said it is always better to do a few things well than many things badly.*

"Do you think I'm doing too much?" she asked, glancing at the cat on the window ledge. "What is your opinion, Jam? Do you think I've ventured too far from shore and am in danger of getting in over my head?"

The little cat lifted her head and looked at Vi. Then she moved a front paw ever so delicately, lowered her head, and resumed her midday nap.

Vi chuckled at Jam's disinterest. The old chair squeaked as Vi sat up, pulled the chair close to the desk, and shoved the ledger into its slot in the back of the desktop—where it belonged. After some minutes, the desk was tidy again.

Something Amiss

Deciding that preparation was the best way to avoid more mishaps, she took a piece of paper and a wooden pencil and commenced making a list of everything that required her attention. At the top of the page, she wrote down what she thought of as easy tasks. Quickly she listed these items: *sewing machine, elevator, order more coal, thank-you note to Dr. and Mrs. Lansing, map for schoolroom.* The list grew, and when she'd finished, Vi reviewed it and decided that, all and all, nothing was too difficult. She added one more word — *telephone* — in hopes that Mrs. Lansing might be able to make it a reality. Then she wrote *fire service*, a project she knew could not be accomplished without great effort.

Then she wrote down three names. Next to *Alma*, she put a question mark. She wrote *Tansy and Marigold* and added the word *future*. Finally she wrote *Professor Marcus Darius Raymond*. Was there a word or a mark to indicate what she needed to do in regard to the professor?

She stared at his name and wondered how she could summarize the tumble of feelings it elicited. A bit of verse from one of her favorite poets, Robert Browning, flashed into her mind: "My whole heart rises up to bless/ Your name in pride and thankfulness!"

A rapping at the door startled her so that she dropped her pencil to the floor.

Mrs. O'Flaherty looked in and said, "Mr. Fredericks's students have been fed and sent on their way. The food baskets are being delivered, and our good friends from the church have departed. Our own lunch is being served." Then she paused, and a grin that showed a flash of gold lifted her entire face.

"Oh, I nearly forgot," Mrs. O added with obvious mirth. "Our special guest has arrived, and I've invited him to share our simple fare."

Violet's Perplexing Puzzles

Though Vi intended to be calm and collected, her heart was pounding as she entered the meeting room. Everyone was seated, but Professor Raymond was instantly on his feet to greet Vi. He hurried to hold Mrs. O'Flaherty's chair and then Vi's. (Without consulting one another, the mission residents had arranged themselves about the table so that the professor was seated next to Vi.)

Polly, who sat beside Mrs. O'Flaherty, pulled at her sleeve and asked in a whisper, "Why did Mr. Professor do that with the chairs?"

Mrs. O leaned down and said, "It is customary for gentlemen to help ladies be seated. But at Samaritan House, we women seat ourselves at our daily meals. That's because Enoch is our only gentleman. Just imagine how tired he would be if he had to hold the chairs of all us women at every meal."

She gave Polly a little wink, and with a giggle, Polly said, "He'd be huffing and puffing all the time."

It was Emily's turn to say the blessing, and she made a point of asking the Lord to grant the professor a safe journey home. Then everyone began eating.

Vi turned to the professor and asked, "Was your meeting productive?"

"Very," he said. "The real estate agent showed me several houses that would be suitable. There were two that I liked particularly, and both are quite close to India Bay University."

"Then you have decided to take the position at the University," Emily said, drawing a logical conclusion from his remarks about looking at houses.

Something Amiss

"I am very tempted," the professor replied, avoiding a direct answer. A little too quickly, he asked, "How is our friend Miss Moran?"

"She's well at present," Emily said, "but naturally worried about how to replace her kitchen. She came to the clinic yesterday and told me that she has already been forced to lower her rents. I'm afraid the stress may make her ill."

"I'm sorry to hear that," said the professor. "She's a nice woman. Is there no one who can help her?"

"That's the problem," Vi said. "There are dozens of Miss Morans in Wildwood, and countless more who have far less than she. How does one help them all?"

This led to a discussion about the problems of housing in Wildwood. Everyone had at least one story of families who had been driven into the streets by fire or loss of their meager incomes. The professor listened closely and asked some pointed questions.

By the time the meal ended, he had a much clearer understanding of the difficulty of sheltering people.

The residents were about to leave the table when the professor asked them to remain for a moment.

"Tomorrow, I must return to the East," he began. "But I couldn't leave without thanking all of you for your kindness to me. I'm a scholar. I dig into the past. But here at Samaritan House, seeing the work you do, the scholar has learned a valuable lesson. The past cannot be altered, but the present—the present can be changed, for better or for worse. Last night, I found myself thinking of something William Shakespeare wrote: 'What's past is prologue.'"

He halted, and a smile came to his face. "I'm sounding too much like a pompous professor, aren't I? Let me just say how much I appreciate all of you. I now know how others must feel when they enter your door — welcomed, valued, and safe."

He looked at Mary, saying, "And superbly fed. I'd gladly travel a day's journey for a bowl of your chicken and dumplings."

At these words, Mary did something no one had seen before. She blushed like a ripe peach, and Vi suddenly realized how much Mary looked like her lovely daughter.

"This is a house of the Lord," the professor concluded, "as great as any cathedral, as glorious as any temple. Never doubt yourselves. Remind yourselves often that you are making change for the better. I think you may even have made a change in me."

No one spoke until Mrs. O'Flaherty said, "Wherever your future takes you, Professor Raymond, our house is always open to you. You have been a good friend to us, and — and —" Her voice broke.

"And a good Samaritan," declared Polly. "That's right, isn't it, Mrs. O?"

"Just right, Polly," said Mrs. O'Flaherty with a laugh.

She laid her napkin on the table and continued, "And now we must get back to the work of being Samaritans." She looked at Alma, and switching to German, she said, "Are you ready for our visit to the dry goods store, my dear? I shall tell you what the professor has said, though not with his eloquence."

Alma had not understood the professor, but she'd seen how his words touched everyone at the table.

The others began telling the professor how glad they were to know him and how much they hoped he might choose to live in India Bay. Alma heard their laughter and good cheer as she followed Mrs. O'Flaherty to the entry hall to get their coats. She was almost afraid to know what the professor had said, for it was certain to remind her of the loving hearts and generous spirits of the people of Samaritan House. Her own heart was torn with confusion and worry, and she couldn't bear another reminder of how she might be hurting her new friends.

CHAPTER

12

The Professor's Request

*He will call upon me, and
I will answer him...*

PSALM 91:15

The Professor's Request

*M*rs. O'Flaherty and Alma left on their errand, and everyone else reluctantly went to their duties. Polly, however, stayed behind, waiting until only Vi and the professor remained in the meeting room. Shyly, she approached Mark Raymond and tugged at his jacket.

Looking down, he said, "It's my young friend Polly! Did you think I'd leave without telling you good-bye?"

He bent forward, lifted Polly up, and stood her upon the dining table. It was a swift, flying motion that made the little girl laugh out loud.

"Now we stand eye to eye," the professor said with a grin. "When I see my own children, I will tell them all about you. I will tell them all about my young friend who makes such lovely pictures and tells such exciting stories. Maybe you can meet them someday."

"Are you coming back to live here?" Polly asked, her bright eyes widening with excitement. "Your children would like it. They could have lots of friends."

The professor stroked his moustache and said, "That's a very good point, Polly. Do you think it is important to have friends?"

"Yes, sir," Polly replied with fervor. "It's very 'portant! I've got Marigold and Tansy, and they're very 'portant to me. You've got friends too, like Miss Vi. She's your special friend, isn't she?"

His voice was oddly gruff as he replied, "Miss Vi is a special person."

Polly grabbed his hand in both of hers and pulled it urgently. "It would make Miss Vi happy if you come back. It would make everybody happy!"

Violet's Perplexing Puzzles

The professor put a finger under Polly's chin and lifted her face. "I'll make you this promise," he said to her. "When I do make my decision, you, Miss Polly Appleton, will be one of the very first people I tell."

Polly's eyes lit up, and she said in amazement, "I will?"

"You will."

Vi heard the door open and turned to see Mary coming in.

"Polly, you've got lessons to do, so tell the professor good-bye," Mary said briskly. She seemed to think there was nothing strange about seeing her daughter standing on the table.

The professor lifted Polly again and swung her down to the floor, earning another delighted laugh.

"Bye, Mr. Professor," Polly said as she ran to her mother.

"She's a terrific little girl," the professor said after Polly was gone. "I don't know how you've done it, Miss Travilla, but all the people you have assembled here at the mission are truly exceptional."

"Don't credit me," Vi said. "I believe that each of us was drawn here for a common purpose. In His infinite wisdom, the Lord brought us together."

"To serve the poor," the professor noted.

"To serve people who are like ourselves," Vi replied. "That is the lesson I have learned. Though their material needs are great, the people of Wildwood are no different from me. And they give me so much more than I can ever give them."

"You said something like that at the Lansings' party, but what is it that the people you help can give to you?" he asked.

"Acceptance," she said, "and friendship. Many people now perceive us as friends—not 'do-gooders' and 'meddlers' as we

were once labeled. I know there are some who still resent our presence, but there has been no repeat of the kind of incidents we experienced in the beginning."

"And no more Mr. Greer?" he questioned.

Vi chuckled softly and said, "From what we've learned, Mr. Greer will not return. There are several outstanding warrants for his arrest—for his forgery and defrauding the courts of South Carolina. I have no fear of him."

"And that hotel owner? I have forgotten his name, but I believe you suspected him of being in league with Mr. Greer," the professor said.

"Mr. Clinch," Vi replied. "I have met him, for he brought Miss Hansen to us. So perhaps I misjudged him."

The professor was studying Vi closely as she spoke, and when she looked into his eyes, she saw the same expression that had so shaken her the previous night. It was as if he were trying to see beyond her face, hunting for something inside her very heart and soul. But this time, his intensity didn't frighten her, and she didn't turn away.

He seemed about to say something when voices broke in. People were coming in the front door—clinic patients, Vi supposed—and their chatter distracted her. She turned, intending to greet them, but the professor grasped her arm.

Repeating the words he'd uttered the night before, he said in a low tone, "I need to speak with you. Is there some place that's private?"

She thought quickly, then said, "The storeroom, on the other side of the entry hall. It used to be a sitting room. It will be empty until Mrs. O and Alma return."

He loosened his hold on her arm and followed her. The visitors were ascending the stairs to the clinic, and they called "hello" to Vi. She saw their curious looks at the tall, sandy-haired gentleman with her, but she merely returned their greetings and proceeded to the storeroom.

The room was cluttered with boxes and clothing. Vi explained that it was Alma's workroom, as she cleared items from two chairs. She sat down and motioned the professor to do the same.

He sat and began to speak: "As I told Polly, I've nearly made up my mind about moving to India Bay. Only two questions remain."

"Your children?" Vi asked.

"If I come, I want them with me, but I cannot force such a change on them. They know nothing of this as yet, and that is why I have cut my visit here short. From here, I will go to Boston. I have to talk with my children and find out how they feel. I think they are happy with their aunt, so I'm not sure what their answer will be."

He lowered his head and clasped his hands together so tightly that his knuckles showed white.

"That is pitiful, isn't it? I am their father, yet I do not know if they will want to live with me. But I hope—"

He stopped speaking suddenly and stood up. He turned away from Vi. Then just as suddenly, he turned back.

"The professor does not even know his own children's thoughts and feelings," he said with a dark laugh. "I have failed them miserably. Here, perhaps, I may be able to redeem myself…to be the father they need. But I don't know if—"

Again he broke off in mid-sentence. He shook his head sadly and paced a few steps.

His suffering was so clear now that Vi could feel his pain as if it were her own.

"You can be what they need," she declared, "because what they need is *you*, Professor Raymond." Her voice quavered with emotion, but it was not weak. "Your children need their father, and it matters not whether you are in Boston or India Bay or — or — Timbuktu!"

He looked at her and said, "You speak with passion."

Vi flushed and looked away. "I have no right to advise you, sir," she said stiffly. "I'm not a parent, but I am a daughter. And my own experience teaches me that what children really need is to know that they are loved."

"But I am so often away from them," he said in a sorrowful tone.

"Then you must make the most of the time you are together," Vi replied. "Children are far more understanding than you may think. Separations will always be difficult, but not nearly so hard when children know that they are truly loved and that even when you are away, they are always in your heart. I have seen how much you love your children, but do they know your feelings, Professor?"

He lowered his head again and didn't reply for several moments.

"I don't have an answer," he said at last.

"Then isn't that question more important than whether you should move to India Bay?" Vi asked. "Isn't that the subject you should discuss with them?"

The professor sat down again. "I have avoided talking about my feelings since my wife died," he said softly. "I told myself that it would be too hurtful for the children, but I was really avoiding my own sorrow. I've buried myself in my work. It seemed the surest way to protect myself from the pain of feeling and to protect my children from my pain."

"But feelings, even painful ones, are God's gift," Vi said with great intensity. "When my father died, I tried to hide my feelings from my family and even from our Lord. It was a dark and frightening time for me. It was only when I finally let my feelings out—shared them unreservedly with God and with my Mamma—that I could begin to make sense of them. I was still a child, yet those feelings were very powerful. Have you considered that your children are suffering from emotions as strong as your own?"

She paused for a moment, fearing that she was saying too much, going too far. But the professor was looking at her with an openness that invited her to continue.

So she said, "It seems to me that your children have suffered a double loss, their mother's death and their father's absence. I know that you are kind and good to them. Yet you say you have avoided discussing your feelings with them. Does that include grief for their mother? As young as they were, they surely loved her as dearly as you did. In trying to protect them, is it possible you denied them what they needed most—the sharing of their grief?"

The professor dropped his head and said, "But it is too late now. Years too late."

"No, it isn't!" Vi exclaimed with a fervor that she could not contain. "It is never too late to open our hearts to the Lord and seek His forgiveness. You believe that, don't you?"

"Yes, I do," the professor said.

"Then let Him be your model," Vi said. "He always shows us the way if we are willing to see and listen. Our

Heavenly Father never abandons us. In happiness and in sorrow, He never lets us down."

"But I have let Him down by failing my children," the professor said.

"Maybe, but just because you have followed the wrong path before, should you take it again? You are a scholar and a scientist. If you conducted an experiment that repeatedly failed, wouldn't you try another approach? You have said that you've failed your children. If that's true, shouldn't you try something different?"

A strange expression came to his face. Several minutes passed in silence, and Vi could almost see his mind at work, turning over ideas. He stood, but he no longer seemed weighted down.

At last he responded: "What you've said—it is as if you have shown me a wall that blocks my progress. I've been running into that wall since the day I learned of my wife's death. Now I see that I must find another way to scale it or go around it."

"I only spoke some words," Vi said. "God is the way. Let Him help you and your children."

He smiled and said, "I thank God for your words, Miss Travilla. It has been many years since someone dared to lecture me. All these years since my wife died, I have said my prayers and read my Bible, but I have done so as a habit empty of meaning. I'd forgotten the comfort of truly opening my thoughts and, yes, my feelings to the Lord. I am sure now that He led me to India Bay that I might have the chance to recover myself."

Vi smiled in return, the dimpled smile that was always a sign of her happiness. "Then India Bay University's offer to you was providential," she said.

"I wasn't thinking of the University," he said. "I was thinking of you. I said there are two questions I must resolve before making my decision. The first is my children, and I must go to Boston to learn their feelings. The second question sits before me."

For a moment, Vi didn't understand what he was saying. "What do you mean, Professor?" she asked.

"You, Miss Travilla," he replied. "I can only accept the University's offer if I know that you approve."

"But of course, I approve. The University position is a great opportunity for you," she declared. "Everyone here will welcome you and your family into the community."

"I find that I only care about one welcome," he said. "I want to know that you will allow me to call on you. I won't use the word 'courtship,' for it may not come to that. I have great affection for you, and I want to know that I may have some hope that it is returned.

"Oh, I am clumsy at this," he said with a frown. "The truth is that I want to see more of you and know more about you" (he'd almost said "everything about you"), and I hope you wish the same."

Vi was blushing, but she was no longer puzzled by his meaning. A sense of pure joy flooded through her.

"I would be happy for you to call on me if you want," she said.

His frown instantly vanished, replaced by the broad, slightly lopsided smile that, to Vi's eyes, was the most handsome smile in the world.

He held out his hand, and she placed her hand lightly upon his palm. As his fingers closed over hers, she felt the

warmth and gentleness in his touch. She rose from her chair, but the professor did not release his grasp.

"I must go now," he said, "but I believe with all my heart that I shall return—permanently. With God's help, I will put my family together again, and we will be able to make a life together—a good life for them and for me. If all goes as I now hope it may, I shall see you in the spring."

"That is not far away," Vi said.

"No, not far away," he responded in a near-whisper. "And I have a great deal of work to do in the meantime. I have a family to rebuild."

"That's all that matters now," Vi said, and in spite of her personal feelings, she meant it. Her heart was with him and the three children in Boston.

"May I write to you?" he asked.

"Yes, please. I feel"—she hesitated—"I want to be of help to you if I can."

He leaned forward, as if, perhaps, to kiss her forehead. But suddenly he stepped back and dropped her hand. From the hallway they'd both heard voices. It was Mrs. O'Flaherty and Alma.

The professor took a watch from his pocket and opened its cover.

"I really must go, for I ordered a cab to come at this time. It's probably here, though I wish I could send it away," he said, earning another of Vi's dimpled smiles.

"You could stay for supper," she suggested.

"Duty calls, I'm afraid. I am dining with Professor Kincaid and his wife tonight," he explained. "He is determined that I shall replace him at the University, and I think he wants to convince me with more reasons why I must come to India Bay. Little does he know that I need no more convincing."

The door opened, and Alma entered. "*Ich bettle Ihre Verzeihung!* I beg your pardon!" the startled girl cried in her native language. She began to back out of the room, but Vi told her to come in.

"I am just leaving," the professor told Alma in his excellent German. "I am very pleased to have met you, Miss Hansen. I hope you will be happy at Samaritan House. You could not be among better people."

"I know, sir," Alma said softly. "They are very good to me."

The professor bowed to her and said farewell. Then he and Vi left to find Mrs. O'Flaherty, for the professor wanted to tell her good-bye.

***

Alma crossed the storeroom, went to the window, and pulled back the lace curtain. She was staring at the bare trees in the yard when a horse and buggy pulled up to the front of the house. After a minute or two, Vi, Mrs. O'Flaherty, and the nice professor emerged in the driveway. If Alma had not been so deep in her own thoughts, she might have seen the glow in Vi's complexion. She might have noticed the professor's rather sheepish expression as he shook Vi's hand and then climbed into the carriage. She might have wondered why Vi lingered in the cold, looking toward the mission gates well after the carriage was gone.

But Alma's mind barely registered what her eyes saw. Her own words came back to her: "They are very good to me." Tears filled her eyes and flowed down her pale cheeks.

The Professor's Request

In anger and desperation, she asked herself why she had let Vi and Mrs. O invite her into Samaritan House. It would have been better if she had never met these caring people. It would have been better if she'd never come to America. Then she would not have to do what she must do. Yet if she refused to follow Mr. Clinch's orders—

The thoughts that hammered at her were so horrible, so frightening that they made her head swim. She felt weak. Her legs almost gave way beneath her. She needed to sit down, but darkness was closing in around her. She extended her arm, grabbing for a chair, but her hand lacked the strength to hold on. Her fingers scraped the wooden chair as she fell forward and collapsed onto the floor.

CHAPTER

13

A Painful Confession

Therefore confess your sins to each other and pray for each other so that you may be healed.

JAMES 5:16

A Painful Confession

Vi and Mrs. O'Flaherty were in the entry hall when they heard a thud followed by a crash. They looked at each other in surprise; then Mrs. O said, "The storeroom."

Vi bounded across the entry hall, Mrs. O'Flaherty close behind. Opening the door, Vi scanned the room. Her eyes traveled toward the window at the front end of the room, and she noticed an overturned chair. Near it lay what appeared to be a bundle of clothing, but Vi recognized the pattern of the material.

"It's Alma!" she cried, rushing to the fallen girl. "Get Emily!"

Mrs. O'Flaherty turned on her heel and ran to summon the nurse.

Vi had gotten to her knees and was holding Alma's wrist. The girl was a deathly white, and her skin felt cold and clammy under Vi's fingers. But Vi found her pulse and knew she was alive. Vi didn't move the girl, but seeing a box of bed linens, she got a coverlet and spread it over Alma. She didn't know what else to do, so she knelt on the floor again and gently stroked Alma's cold hand.

Emily was soon at her side, and Vi moved to let the capable nurse take over. Emily felt Alma's pulse, pronouncing it slow but steady. Then she carefully examined Alma's head, looked into her eyes, and felt her limbs.

"She's fainted," Emily said. "There's a scrape on her cheek, probably where she hit the floor. There's no sign of concussion, and I can find nothing else."

She reached into the pocket of her crisp apron and removed a little bottle of smelling salts. Uncorking it, she began to move the bottle slowly back and forth under Alma's nose. In a few seconds, the girl's eyelids fluttered. She awoke with a gasp and tried to push Emily's hand away.

"You're all right now, Alma," Emily said in a soothing way. "You fainted. Now take a few moments to rest, and then I'll help you sit up. There now. Slowly does it."

Ever so gently, Emily slipped her arms under Alma's shoulders and assisted her. Vi was glad to see some color coming into Alma's face, though she was still abnormally pale, and she was shivering. The coverlet had fallen to the floor, so Vi found a woolen shawl and wrapped it around the girl. When Alma said that she was feeling better, Vi and Emily helped her to her feet and to the chair where Professor Raymond had sat.

Emily continued to minister to her patient, feeling her brow for fever (there was none) and then listening to her heart with a stethoscope.

"I think you're fine," Emily said, "but I want to keep an eye on you. We'll help you upstairs to the clinic. You will be more comfortable in a bed rather than on the floor," she added with a smile.

Alma looked to Vi, who quickly translated Emily's words. Mrs. O'Flaherty was standing in the doorway, and Enoch — who had been in the kitchen and heard the commotion — stood with her. Emily motioned to Enoch, but when he approached, Alma drew back and cried out, "*Nein!* No! No!"

These were the first words she'd spoken, and they stopped Enoch in mid-step.

"Don't be afraid," Vi said in Alma's language. "Enoch is very strong. He can carry you with ease. And I'll be right with you."

A Painful Confession

Alma's voice rose, and she clutched Vi's hand. "I am not afraid of Enoch. But I must talk to you and Mrs. O. Just the two of you. I must talk to you now. Please, Miss Vi, now!"

Vi looked up at Emily and briefly told her what Alma had said.

"I don't know what caused her to faint, but it could be this anxiety," Emily replied. "If there is something troubling her, it might help her to speak of it. Enoch and I will wait outside. Just call us if she seems faint again."

The nurse motioned to Enoch, and they left the room. Mrs. O'Flaherty retrieved the fallen chair and brought it to Alma's side. Vi found a small stool and sat down near Alma's feet.

"Now then, we're alone," Mrs. O'Flaherty said in the gentlest of tones. "Whatever it is, you can speak freely to us."

Alma's head dropped forward, and she said sorrowfully, "I must tell you, even though you will hate me."

"Oh, no!" Vi protested in English. Switching to German, she said, "We love you, Alma. You're part of our family now, and nothing can make us hate you."

"But you will," Alma said, lifting her tear-filled eyes to Vi. "And I will understand."

Mrs. O'Flaherty removed a handkerchief from her sleeve and gave it to Alma. As the girl was wiping her eyes, there was a soft knock at the door. Emily came in and handed a cup and saucer to Mrs. O.

"See if you can get her to drink this," Emily said.

185

Violet's Perplexing Puzzles

Mrs. O'Flaherty nodded, and Emily quickly left.

"You must try to drink some tea," Mrs. O told Alma. "It will help you get your strength back."

She put the cup in the girl's hands, and Alma took a few sips. Then she gave the cup back to the older woman, and she made an effort to smile as she said, "*Danke.* Thank you.

"Now I must tell you of a terrible thing," Alma began in her native language. With obvious effort, she sat up in the chair and drew a deep breath.

"I have been dishonest with you," she said slowly. "You took me in without question, and I have betrayed your trust."

Vi glanced questioningly at Mrs. O'Flaherty, but Mrs. O was equally mystified and could reply only with a slight shrug of her shoulders.

"It can't be so bad," Vi said, putting her hand over Alma's. "And you will feel better if you tell us."

"Bad it is," Alma responded tearfully. "I took your ledger. I did it because Mr. Clinch told me to. Last Saturday, I took a walk and went to the hotel because he had made me promise to. I thought he wanted only to see that I was well, but he told me to find your record book in your office. I had to take it to him, and then I brought it back. Mr. Clinch said it was not stealing, only borrowing. But in my heart, I knew better. Today he tells me to do something else bad."

"You saw him today?" Mrs. O'Flaherty asked.

"When you and I left the dry goods store, you went to the grocer's, and I waited on the walkway. Mr. Clinch came out of his hotel and found me there. He acted like he wanted to be pleasant to me, but he was telling me what he wants," Alma said.

"And what was that?" Vi asked.

186

A Painful Confession

"It made no sense to me. He wants information about Miss Emily and Dr. Bowman and the professor. He wants to know about their families and where they live and if they are married. I asked why, but he said it was none of my business. Oh, Miss Vi, he also ordered me to search your bedroom and bring him any personal letters I can find. I can't do that! Mr. Clinch can do the worst thing to me, and still I cannot do that to you!"

Alma had started to weep again, but with determination, she dashed at her wet cheeks with her hand, flinching when she touched the raw scrape on her face.

"Don't worry about the ledger," Vi said. "I don't know why he wanted it, but I'm sure it was a disappointment to him. Has he given you any reason for his strange requests?"

Alma sniffed and replied, "No. Except he did say something that I didn't understand. He said, 'Trust can be broken. People like to believe the worst of others.' What people was he talking about?"

"I don't know," Vi admitted.

Alma went on, "He does not want the mission here. When I was working for him, I heard him say so many times. My English is very poor, but I understand more words than he knows. And I could see how angry he was when he talked about the mission."

"Whom did he talk with about the mission?" Mrs. O'Flaherty asked in German.

"Some other men like him. They own hotels and saloons, and they are bad men. They make me scared."

"Well, they can't harm you here," Vi said firmly. "You are safe with us."

Touching Alma's hand, Vi asked, "I think Mr. Clinch has threatened you in some way, hasn't he?"

 187

Violet's Perplexing Puzzles

Alma lowered her head again and said, "He's knows something that he promises to tell me if I do what he commands. Mr. Clinch knows where my brother is. I don't know how he found out, but he is very clever. He promises to tell me where Rudy is and to help me make a reunion with my darling brother. But Mr. Clinch says I must pay for this information first. Since I have no money, he says I must pay by doing favors for him. I did not think he would ask me for anything bad, but when he told me to get the ledger book, I knew he is somehow trying to hurt you and the mission."

"Blackmail!" said Mrs. O'Flaherty with an angry glower. "Blackmail and intimidation. I never liked Mr. Clinch, but I didn't imagine him capable of such low tricks as to threaten the happiness of a trusting young woman like you, Alma. None of this is your fault, my child. You must believe that. You have been caught in his vile scheme, just as he hopes to ensnare me and Vi and everyone at the mission. He's a clever man. But he did not count on the honesty and bravery of our Alma."

Alma's head popped up, and she stared at Mrs. O. "I have been dishonest and cowardly," the girl exclaimed in her native tongue. "I have betrayed all of you! I was thinking only of myself when I took the ledger! I am so ashamed."

"We forgive you for taking the ledger, and I am sure you have asked our Lord for His forgiveness," Mrs. O'Flaherty said in her confident manner. "I believe it was your sense of shame that kept you from accompanying me to church last Sunday."

Alma's eyes softened as she replied, "Yes, it was. I had not taken the ledger book yet, but I was ashamed to enter God's house because I was not being truthful with you. But

A Painful Confession

I was so afraid that I would never find Rudy that I could not tell you the truth. If I could not face you, how could I face God?"

"God above all knows the pain that a repentant sinner feels. He understands what is in our hearts, dear girl, and He knows that you were caught in a terrible situation that was not of your making," Mrs. O'Flaherty said. "Taking the ledger was wrong, but it was a minor thing compared to what Mr. Clinch has done. I know it has weighed very heavily on your conscience, yet how brave you have been to tell us."

"But I lied again, today, to Mr. Clinch," Alma said with downcast eyes. "When he told me to find out about the people here, he also asked a question about you, Mrs. O'Flaherty. It was strange. He asked if you'd ever been an actress. I told him that I knew nothing about your life, but that wasn't true. He is an awful man, but that does not excuse my lying."

Mrs. O'Flaherty had to smile. "God's commandment to us is not to bear false witness. You didn't do that, Alma, and I am sure He will forgive you for omitting to tell Clinch what you do know about me. Remember that He understands your motives as well as your actions. Your motive was to protect your friends here from harm. And I am certainly pleased you think well enough of me not to share my stories with that man."

"Then you do not hate me?" Alma asked shyly.

"Of course not," Mrs. O'Flaherty said with a broad smile. "We love you and value you, don't we, Vi?"

"Of course," Vi said, "and we'll do everything in our power to help you have that reunion with your brother."

"But Mr. Clinch will never tell me where Rudy is," Alma said.

"Don't you believe it," Mrs. O'Flaherty said. "You have not been with us very long, so you do not know about the mysteries we have solved. As detectives, we are quite good at finding lost people and ferreting out secrets. Thanks entirely to you, Alma, we now know that Mr. Clinch is up to something. I am confident we can get the information you need."

"It is most important that he not hurt Samaritan House," Alma said. "That must come first, and you must let me help. Tell me what I can do to make amends for my sin against you."

Vi rose from the stool and extended her hand. "The sin is washed away," she said with a beautiful smile. "Just let us take you to the clinic, so Emily can watch over you. Tomorrow, we'll decide what to do about Mr. Clinch."

Alma took Vi's hand and stood. She was a little wobbly, so Mrs. O'Flaherty clasped her waist, and Vi held her arm. When they left the storeroom, Emily and Enoch were waiting patiently. This time, Alma allowed herself to be carried up the stairs in Enoch's strong arms.

Emily examined Alma once again and then tucked her into a comfortable bed in a cubicle at the rear of the clinic. By the time Emily closed the linen curtain that separated the little space from the main part of the clinic, Alma had fallen asleep—the first truly peaceful sleep she'd had since her arrival in Wildwood.

Downstairs, people were arriving for the afternoon meal, so Vi and Mrs. O'Flaherty had no chance to discuss Alma's revelations. If truth be told, once she was sure that Alma was all right, Vi's mind quickly abandoned the problem of Mr. Clinch and flew to the professor. Some of the regular dinner guests, like old Widow Amos, took special notice of Vi that afternoon—the lightness in her step and the sprightliness of her conversation. Mrs. Amos, in fact, stopped in to see Miss Moran on her way home and happened to mention Miss Travilla.

"She's such a nice young lady," Miss Moran told her friend. "Did I tell you that she sent a carpenter over to make an estimate of the cost of a new kitchen? I don't know what can come of it, though. The fire has made me even poorer than a church mouse."

"I hear her family is real wealthy," Mrs. Amos confided, "but I don't get the idea that she can just hand out money. I'll wager she's workin' on an idea for you—some way to get you back to cookin'. Speakin' of Miss Travilla, I think there's something going on with that girl."

"Whatever do you mean?" asked Miss Moran, leaning closer so that she'd miss nothing Mrs. Amos had to say.

"Not that I really know," Mrs. Amos said. "Just that she was almost dancin' round the room when she served us our meal. And talkin' to everybody in the loveliest way. She had a kinda brightness—what my old mama used to call being moonstruck."

"Like a girl in love?" Miss Moran ventured.

"Just like that," Mrs. Moran nodded. "But you didn't hear it from me."

"Oh, I wouldn't say a word," Miss Moran affirmed.

But she did just happen to say a word—quite a few words—to one of her remaining boarders, who passed it on to a friend, who passed it on to someone else. And that was how gossip spread in Wildwood, just as it does in every corner of the world. Many guesses were made about who could be the object of Miss Travilla's affection. The doctor? The new teacher? The favorite speculation was some unknown gentleman who traveled in social circles high above the realm of Wildwood. Whoever it might be, most people were hopeful that it was someone worthy of the brave young lady's esteem. A number of people began to wonder what would happen to the mission if she up and married so soon after coming to Wildwood. For a few, the gossip shook their newly found hopefulness. So much good was being accomplished at the mission. If Miss Travilla left, how would Samaritan House go on? Would she abandon Wildwood, as others had done before? And what then?

CHAPTER

14

Making a Plan

He who despises his neighbor
sins, but blessed is he who
is kind to the needy.

PROVERBS 14:21

Making a Plan

*E*arly the next morning, Vi and Mrs. O'Flaherty had the first of several conversations about Mr. Clinch and what Alma had told them. It was Friday, so Dr. Bowman and Emily arrived at Samaritan House as the residents were about to have their breakfast. Emily had informed the doctor of Alma's fainting spell, and he immediately went to the clinic to check the girl. To everyone's relief, he declared the young seamstress to be "fit as a fiddle" and released her from her bed.

Indeed, Alma seemed like a different girl when she had dressed and come to the kitchen for some breakfast. There was color in her cheeks, and she looked healthier than they'd ever seen. When Mrs. O'Flaherty remarked on her appearance, Alma said shyly in German, "I think that guilt is like a disease, Mrs. O. It makes one sick in body and spirit. I woke before dawn and talked a long time with my Father in Heaven. I told Him everything, and He has forgiven my sinfulness and healed me of my guilt. I have learned a great lesson."

"I can see that," Mrs. O'Flaherty smiled in reply. Then she asked if Alma would be willing to talk a bit more about what had happened, and the girl readily agreed. She was anxious to make amends, and she wanted to help her friends.

So Alma and Mrs. O'Flaherty met with Vi, Emily, and Dr. Bowman in her office. Alma went through her story again, filling in a few details (that Mr. Clinch spoke passably good German, for example). She also said that she was supposed to see Mr. Clinch again on Sunday morning, while the other mission residents were at church. He had instructed her to come to his back door and to be sure that she was not seen.

In the afternoon, when the clinic hours were over, Vi, Mrs. O, Emily, and the doctor met again, putting their heads together to determine what Mr. Clinch was up to. Emily wondered if they should prepare for more harmful pranks, but Mrs. O'Flaherty had a theory that seemed more plausible. She believed that Mr. Clinch wanted information that he could use against the mission.

"The ledger," Mrs. O'Flaherty said, "would tell him about our finances. I'm sure he now knows who our wealthy donors are. There are a number of influential people who have been generous to Samaritan House."

"You're right," Vi said with obvious concern. "I list every contribution we receive in my ledger—the donors' names, addresses, and the amounts of their gifts. But how does this relate to his questions about all of us?"

"Learning about the people here—well, from small truths, he could concoct great fictions," Mrs. O'Flaherty said. "He gave himself away when he asked if I'd been an actress. That is still regarded as an infamous and immoral profession by many people. He could use information like that to manufacture a scandal by starting a few nasty rumors. You know how gossip spreads. Once a false story is started in Wildwood, then some of the mission's more prominent donors might receive anonymous letters repeating the story and questioning the wisdom of further financial gifts to Samaritan House."

With a bitter laugh, Mrs. O continued, "Imagine if the mayor or some of the pastors of the city's wealthy churches received letters claiming that the poor people of Wildwood were being ministered to by an eccentric lady who had flaunted herself on the musical stage! That's the kind of story he could make up from the tiniest grain of truth."

"A rumor campaign!" exclaimed the doctor, slapping his knee. "It's just the kind of cowardly scheme that man would set in motion. He's as slippery as an eel, ladies. We were never able to connect him to the threatening incidents at the mission last fall, and even the police could not link Clinch to Mr. Greer and the attempt to kidnap Tansy and Marigold. Clinch is too clever to leave evidence of his crimes."

Emily asked what Mr. Clinch hoped to accomplish by spreading false rumors. "We would just deny everything and tell the truth," she said.

"Controlling gossip and rumor is a very difficult task," Mrs. O'Flaherty observed. "Something like trying to dam a stream in the midst of a raging flood. In Proverbs, it says 'A perverse man stirs up dissension, and a gossip separates close friends.' Clinch is certainly perverse, and with gossip and rumor, he may plan to separate us from the people we serve and the people who support our efforts. He can destroy the mission by destroying faith in us—and perhaps our faith in ourselves."

Vi was thinking of something Alma had told them. "Now it makes sense," she said. "Alma didn't comprehend his meaning, but I believe Mr. Clinch revealed his whole plan to her. He told her, 'Trust can be broken. People like to believe the worst of others.'

"What a monstrous man," she went on in a tone cold with anger. "He uses Alma's greatest fear to get information that he can distort into hateful lies, and he counts on human curiosity and gullibility to spread gossip and undermine confidence in Samaritan House. If the people of Wildwood lose their trust in us, everything we have done thus far will be in vain. We cannot let that happen. So, how do we stop Mr. Tobias Clinch?"

At first, it seemed to them that thwarting Mr. Clinch's scheme was an impossible task. But as they debated various ideas, a plan evolved. It must be carried out quickly, for they all agreed that a "rumor campaign," as Dr. Bowman called it, was like a noxious weed: it had to be pulled out before it could take root.

They decided to meet again the next day to refine their plan. In the meantime, Mrs. O'Flaherty would speak with Alma, whose agreement was essential. And Vi would explain everything to the Reeves and Mary. All the residents had roles to play on the coming Sunday if their plan was to succeed.

⟋⟍⟍⟋

Alma was, as Mrs. O'Flaherty expected, eager to participate. In part, she wanted to punish Mr. Clinch, but far more important than vengeance was her desire to protect the people of Samaritan House. In a little more than a week, Alma had come to feel like a member of the Samaritan family. They had welcomed her with open arms, forgiven her without casting blame, and asked nothing in return for their kindness.

The other members of the household were just as anxious to play their roles. They spent longer than usual at their Saturday lunch, going over the details. Enoch, Christine, and Mary made a number of good suggestions, which were incorporated into the plan.

Making a Plan

There was one thing that still worried Vi, and she confided it to Mrs. O'Flaherty that night when they talked before bed.

"I wish I had a chance to consult with Mamma and Ed," she said. "I know we're doing right, but I always seek their counsel on important matters."

"Almost always," Mrs. O'Flaherty chuckled. "I don't recall your consulting them when you rushed alone into Mr. Clinch's hotel and rescued Marigold from the horrible Mr. Greer."

"There wasn't time," Vi protested.

"That's the point, Vi girl," said Mrs. O, her expression becoming serious. "You're an adult now, and you've taken on adult responsibilities. With God's guidance, you must learn to trust your own decisions. I'm not saying you shouldn't consult your mother and brother when you can. An adult will always seek knowledge and advice from wiser heads when she needs to. But that isn't always possible. In this situation, we have agreed that we must act quickly in order to stop a grievous harm from being done. We have thought it through. We've considered other options. We have decided on a course that will not put anyone in physical jeopardy, even if the plan should go wrong. Do you believe that Elsie or Ed could do more?"

"Not really," Vi replied. "In fact, I was thinking this afternoon that we are doing exactly as Papa would in these circumstances, just as he did when he stood up against the Ku Klux Klan."

"From what I know of your father, I think you're right," Mrs. O'Flaherty agreed. "You have prayed about what to do. Have you felt any doubts when you talked to the Lord?"

"None at all," Vi said. "I do not doubt that God will be with us tomorrow."

Violet's Perplexing Puzzles

"Then be resolute," Mrs. O'Flaherty said, the smile returning to her face. "Tomorrow we will take justice to Mr. Clinch."

"Do you think he is truly an evil man?" Vi asked.

Mrs. O'Flaherty contemplated this question for some moments. Then she said, "I think Mr. Clinch is a man who has denied himself the knowledge of God. He has cut himself off from the precious love of our Lord and Savior. Mr. Clinch is desperately afraid of losing his little bit of power here in Wildwood, because it is all that he has. Whether he is truly evil, I cannot say, for only God knows the deepest part of anyone's heart. I will say that behind his scheming and lying and his smug smiles, I think Mr. Clinch is a terribly sad and lonely person."

"I think we should include him in our prayers tonight," Vi said suddenly. "Even though he has done his best to hurt us, we can't repay him in kind."

"You remind me of the words of the Apostle Peter: 'Do not repay evil with evil or insult with insult, but with blessing, because to this you were called so that you may inherit a blessing,'" Mrs. O'Flaherty said, quoting 1 Peter 3:9.

Mr. Clinch would surely have been astounded to know that his name was included in anyone's prayers. He would have been even more amazed if he'd known that the person praying on his behalf was Miss Violet Travilla—the young woman whose life's work he was determined to destroy.

CHAPTER

15

Showdown

Therefore be as shrewd as snakes and as innocent as doves.

Showdown

*V*ery early on Sunday morning, a hired cab delivered Emily and Dr. Bowman to the rear entrance of Samaritan House. Several hours later, Enoch drove the mission carriage to the front of the house. Vi, Mrs. O'Flaherty, Christine, and baby Jacob—all dressed in their Sunday outfits— climbed into the vehicle, and the carriage departed. A few minutes later, Mary Appleton and her daughter, wearing their best bonnets, came out of the house and walked down the street in the direction of their church.

The young man watching these activities had arrived at his vantage point too late to see the cab, but everything he did observe appeared perfectly normal. The clerk from the Wildwood Hotel had been sent to spy on the mission, and he was anxious to get in from the cold. So seeing all the residents depart—except for the German girl—he hurried back to report to his boss, Mr. Clinch.

If the clerk had watched for a while longer, he would have been puzzled to see the carriage return with all its passengers, followed by Mary and Polly Appleton on foot. But neither he nor Mr. Clinch had reason to expect such an odd thing.

Inside Samaritan House, Alma was waiting. After a few minutes of consultation, Vi kissed Alma's cheek, and the girl walked out the front door.

Vi looked at her watch. "We leave in five minutes," she said. "I don't want Alma to be alone there for a minute longer than necessary."

With quick steps, Alma hurried down Wildwood Street toward the hotel. When she reached the shopping area, she ducked into an alley that ran beside the hotel and led to the stable. She looked at the stable. Assured, she turned to the right, at the rear of the hotel. A rough timber stairway rose to a small platform and the back door of Mr. Clinch's office.

On the little landing, she stopped to take a few deep breaths and look at the stable once again. Then she opened the door.

"You're late!" barked Mr. Clinch in his crude but understandable German. "Close that door before you chill the whole room."

"Yes, sir," Alma replied in a tremulous tone.

"Don't you start crying on me!" he commanded. "Did anyone see you leave?"

The girl said, "I waited until after they all left for church."

To herself, Alma silently asked God to forgive her for this one half-truth. She looked swiftly about the office, observing that the shade was drawn. The only light came from the desk lamp, which cast an eerie yellow glow over Mr. Clinch's face. He was sitting at his desk and glaring at her sharply.

"Well, warm yourself at the fire," Mr. Clinch said in a more even tone.

She did as she was told and went to the iron stove in the corner. She watched while Mr. Clinch took his money box from its drawer. He opened the box and removed a crisp bill, which he laid on the desk.

"May I hang up my cloak, sir?" Alma asked.

"On the rack outside," he said with impatience. He waved toward the inner door between his office and the

204

hotel's saloon. Hurrying into the barroom, Alma was glad to see that no customers were there. She returned to the office, taking care to leave the door slightly ajar.

Standing before the desk, she waited for Mr. Clinch to speak.

He put his forefinger on the money and said, "If your information is good, this is for you. I hope you are saving your money, Alma. You can use it to buy a train ticket when you go to see your brother."

His voice was honeyed now, and he bestowed on her that seemingly sincere smile, which had once made her trust him without question.

"Then Rudy is not in India Bay?" she asked.

"I don't believe so," he replied with teasing cruelty. "You'd hardly need to travel by train if he were. You must take a trip to see him. But I forgot. You don't know where he is, do you? It would be a shame if you did not learn of his location. The United States is a very large country. You could easily hunt from now until doomsday and never get your brother's scent."

"But you know where he is," she said, anger in her voice. "I could find him if you told me the truth."

Mr. Clinch put his hands up as if to ward off a blow. "Control your temper," he said, sounding like a harsh schoolmaster. "You must earn the knowledge you seek. Right now, I want your information about those mission people, and then I have a new assignment for you. When you've done all that I require, then you will get your truth."

Alma lowered her head and said, "I understand. I have learned some things."

She told him a number of innocent facts about the doctor, Miss Clayton, and Mrs. O'Flaherty—information they had all agreed she should convey.

Violet's Perplexing Puzzles

When she finished, Mr. Clinch was frowning darkly. "There's nothing in what you tell me that I can use," he said with irritation. "But did you get Miss Travilla's personal mail?"

Alma dug into her pocket and pulled out several letters. She handed them to Mr. Clinch. He shuffled through the envelopes, noting the different handwriting on each. His expression didn't change, but his voice was actually pleasant when he said, "I'll read these letters now, so you can return them to the mission before Miss Travilla has time to miss them. Wait in the saloon. I'll call you when I've finished."

Alma went back to the saloon and smiled as she looked about her. Not two minutes had passed before an angry bellow, like the roar of a bull, issued from the office.

"Alma!" he shouted. "Get back here!"

Alma didn't move, but her smile grew wider.

Mr. Clinch shouted for her again, and then came loud scraping and bumping sounds as if furniture were being tossed aside. Something crashed, and the door was flung open.

Mr. Clinch stood in the doorway. His face was a dark crimson, and his eyes almost bulged with his rage. He clutched a piece of paper in his fist, and he raised his arm as if to lash out physically. He was shouting in English, "You stupid, ignorant girl! You—"

His words were cut short by the sight in front of his eyes. Alma was standing a few feet away. No longer the shy, frightened girl, she stood straight and proud, and a look of defiance flashed in her eyes. To her right was Dr. Bowman, and on her left were Vi and Mrs. O'Flaherty.

Clinch could not believe his eyes. He looked from one to another of the mission people before him, and his fierce gaze settled on Vi.

"Hello, Mr. Clinch," she said as naturally as if she were merely greeting him in passing. "We've come to collect Miss Hansen and escort her home."

Clinch's mind was whirring. From the innocent tone of Vi's voice, he guessed that perhaps these people had just arrived and had not heard his incriminating conversation with Alma. Maybe, he thought, he could redeem this situation after all.

Forcing himself to smile, the hotel owner said, "Forgive my shouting, Miss Travilla. Miss Hansen left before I could give her a little gift, and I merely wanted to stop her departure."

"Oh, really," Vi said with a large dose of sarcasm. "Perhaps you have something to give me as well."

Clinch looked at her quizzically, as though he had no idea what she meant.

Vi took a step forward, and she continued, "Let's not play games, Mr. Clinch. We know what you are trying to do, and it is abominable that you should try to include Miss Hansen in your plotting. You judged her quite wrongly. She is a good person with a strong conscience. She told us everything, and she bravely volunteered to help us carry out our own plan."

Clinch didn't know what to say. Like all bullies, he was unaccustomed to having any of his victims confront him. Facing the tall young woman with the riveting dark eyes, his impulse was to flee. Hoping to find sanctuary in his office — and escape through his back door if these mission people tried to follow him — he turned quickly, only to bang into the powerful figure of Enoch Reeve, who was blocking the office doorway behind him.

Enoch placed his large hands on the hotel owner's shoulders and turned Mr. Clinch around as easily as he might spin the cap off a jar of applesauce. Enoch maintained his hold on Clinch, forcing the man to face Vi and the others. Clinch attempted to shake Enoch's strong grip, but his efforts were useless.

With amusement, Enoch said, "It's discourteous to leave without excusing yourself, sir. Just calm down now, and pay good attention to what Miss Violet has to tell you."

"We wouldn't send Miss Hansen here alone," Vi continued. "Mr. Reeve took another route to your back door. He has been here the whole time, as have we. I heard everything you said to Miss Hansen. Now it's my turn to speak. We know what you want to do to hurt the mission. It is surprising that a man of your age would stoop to something as childish as spreading lies and rumors to harm others. If you were to execute your scheme, it would certainly cause us problems. But it would not drive us away, Mr. Clinch. It would never have worked."

Clinch opened his mouth, but he could think of nothing to say. The possibility of escaping was cut off, so he could only stand where he was—dumbfounded and slack-jawed.

"I hope you are listening carefully to me, for I have a proposal to make," Vi went on. "Now, we could take this matter to the police. They might not be able to prosecute you for your blackmail of Miss Hansen, but I believe there is a law against coercing another person to commit a crime, like the theft of my personal property. I see that you have one of my letters in your hand even now. In any case, I feel certain that the police would appreciate having an excuse to investigate your activities closely. Your business here might suffer, for it's unlikely your customers would feel comfortable in the presence of the officers of the law."

"But—but you can't—" Clinch stammered.

"She can," Dr. Bowman said in a hard tone, "and she will. Trust me, Mr. Clinch. We can make life very difficult for you. There are people at the highest levels of government who would like nothing better than to clean out the saloons and gambling dens of Wildwood."

"That's blackmail!" Clinch exclaimed.

"You would know," Mrs. O'Flaherty said with a snorting laugh. "But no, it isn't blackmail. We want nothing tangible from you, Mr. Clinch."

"That's right," Vi said. "We only want you to change your behavior. You might say that we have come to offer you a truce. You must accept one fact—Samaritan House is here to stay. Much as we might like to, we have no intention of interfering with your business. Our purpose is to follow our Lord by serving others. We want to help those who need help. And we will share His message with all who enter our doors. But if people choose to forsake your bar and your gambling tables, that will be their choice."

"You want to ruin me," Clinch said miserably.

"You don't need us for that. You are perfectly capable of ruining yourself," Mrs. O'Flaherty responded.

"As I said, we're here to stay," Vi went on, her voice a little softer. "If you cannot accept that fact, you are not as intelligent as I thought. If you cannot live in peace with us, then I assure you that we will fight for our right to be here and carry on our work with the people of Wildwood. You and your cronies must leave us alone, Mr. Clinch, and we will leave you alone."

Clinch was a smart man, and he knew when he was defeated. It would do him no good to protest his innocence or make false excuses. These "do-gooders" had figured out his scheme, he realized, and they would not be driven out. If he didn't agree to their truce, it was he who would suffer.

"All right," he said in resignation. "I accept your offer. My *cronies*, as you call my fellow businessmen, will do as I say. Is that all you want?"

"Yes," Vi said. But in the next instant, she changed her answer. "No. I want to know everything that you know about the whereabouts of Miss Hansen's brother. Or was that another lie?"

"I do know," Clinch said. "I will give you his address. It's in my office."

Vi grasped Alma's hand and smiled brilliantly. Alma had understood little of what was being said, but she instinctively knew that Vi had somehow gotten Mr. Clinch to reveal his information about Rudy.

To Clinch, Vi said, "I also want your promise not to impede Miss Hansen in reuniting with her brother. It would be a petty kind of revenge on us, and I guarantee that any further effort to cause us harm would have unpleasant consequences for you."

"I know that," Clinch said with the bitterness of a man who had no other options.

"And you will return Miss Travilla's letters," Dr. Bowman added. "Not that they were much help to you. Here, give me the one that you are holding."

Clinch held out the wad of paper in his hand. The doctor looked at the crumpled sheet and grinned. All but one of the letters they had supplied for Clinch were merely social notes — thank-you letters and invitations. But this sheet, put into an envelope that once contained a message from Mrs. Lansing, had been written by the doctor himself. It was just a single sentence that had provoked Clinch's bellowing rage and precipitated the confrontation. It read: "Aren't you ashamed of yourself, Mr. Clinch?"

———

With Enoch at his side, Clinch went into his office and opened a drawer in his desk. He took out a letter and handed it to Alma. The letter was from Rudy Hansen himself. Grudgingly, Clinch explained how he had come to know Alma's brother.

In search of work, Rudy had traveled to India Bay when he first came to the United States, and being able to afford little better, he had stayed briefly at the Wildwood Hotel. He'd written to Alma while he was there, giving her the hotel's address. That had eventually led Alma to the hotel, but by the time she arrived, Rudy had gone to California — lured by the stories of the American West and the fortunes to be made there.

Clinch had promised to contact Rudy if his sister ever came to the hotel. Rudy's letter, written before Christmas, inquired if Clinch had any news of Alma and reminded the hotel owner of his promise. The letter included Rudy's address in San Francisco, where the young German immigrant had found steady employment as a dock worker at that city's busy wharves. The letter made it clear how worried Rudy was about Alma and how much he wanted his sister to join him.

Rudy had written in English, and Mrs. O'Flaherty translated the letter for Alma. The girl flushed with joy, and tears flowed from her eyes as she listened.

Watching this scene, the hotel owner said through clenched teeth, "Does she ever stop her infernal weeping?"

Violet's Perplexing Puzzles

Hearing his remark, Vi said, "Those are tears of relief and gladness, Mr. Clinch. In spite of yourself, you have at last fulfilled your promises to Rudy and Alma. Can you find no satisfaction in this deed? Don't you feel some happiness in being the instrument—albeit unintentional—of such joy as Alma's?"

Clinch looked at Vi. She thought she saw some confusion in his eyes, and his expression seemed to soften slightly. But after a few seconds, he sputtered out a gruff "Bah!" and turned away from Vi's gaze.

"We'll be leaving now," she said, not unkindly. "We will be on our guard, but if you keep your end of the bargain, there will be no need for another meeting like this. Keep the truce, Mr. Clinch."

Mrs. O'Flaherty, Alma, and the doctor had left the dark office. Vi said, "I hope you find peace, Mr. Clinch. I truly do." Then she too departed.

Enoch was the last to go. But at the doorway, he stopped and turned back to Clinch with a warning: "You best heed Miss Vi's words, sir, because I'll be watching your every move. A wise man would think about what she said, about finding peace. You won't find it in this place for sure. It's in your heart, if you got the sense to let the good Lord come in and clean away your sins."

Then Enoch was gone, and Tobias Clinch was left alone with his thoughts.

***

Reverend and Mrs. Stephens had worried when no one from Samaritan House attended church. So they decided to call at the mission to check that the residents were all right. What they found was a celebration.

Vi explained what had occurred and why. When she finished, Reverend Stephens said, "Now I understand your celebratory mood. No one before you ever dared to confront Mr. Clinch directly. You must surely have 'put on the full armor of God' and taken your stand against the devil's schemes, as it says in Ephesians."

"Oh, we aren't celebrating our confrontation with Mr. Clinch," Vi said. "Thanks be to God, we prevailed, and I am confident that Samaritan House is saved from his spiteful plot. But it isn't easy to see a man so humbled. No, we are celebrating the finding of Alma's brother."

"We have written a message to him, which Enoch will take to the telegraph office tomorrow morning," Emily said.

"I'll be at the door when it opens," Enoch grinned.

"I am so happy for you, Alma," Mrs. Stephens said with tears glistening in her eyes. "I am sure that you and your brother will be together again soon. In fact, I know you will, for the people of Samaritan House will see that it happens."

"Thank you," Alma replied in heavily accented English. Then she added something in German.

Mrs. O'Flaherty translated: "Alma would like to know if she may attend your church next Sunday. She says that she has missed her visits to God's house."

Mrs. Stephens reached across the table and patted Alma's hand. "You are more than welcome," the kind lady said. "We would be honored to have a young lady as courageous as you join our congregation."

Alma nodded her head and said in her hesitant English, "Very much would I like to come next Sunday."

The minister and his wife left soon after. At Vi's request, they agreed not to tell anyone about what Mr. Clinch had done.

Violet's Perplexing Puzzles

"We all decided to keep it to ourselves," Vi explained. "We think Mr. Clinch deserves the opportunity to be judged by his actions. The whole thing was humiliating for him, and we don't want to add to his burden."

"I'm heartened by your compassion," Reverend Stephens said before he and his wife departed. "It takes strength not to gloat when one is the victor. Perhaps this experience will shine the light into Mr. Clinch's heart."

"I pray that will happen," Vi said.

The rest of the day passed in a lovely spirit of peacefulness and calm. Samaritan House had survived another threat. For this reason, Vi decided to change the text she'd chosen for their devotion. She substituted Proverbs 3:33: "The LORD's curse is on the house of the wicked, but he blesses the home of the righteous."

The discussion that followed focused on the home they were creating at Samaritan House and the difference in meaning between a house and a home.

Little Polly expressed it simply in a way that touched all their hearts.

"A house is a building," she said, "but a home is a place where you feel safe and loved. Thank You, Jesus, for saving our home. It's called Samaritan *House,* but it's really a home."

They all prayed with grateful hearts, and Vi made a point of naming Tobias Clinch when she asked for God's blessing on all the people of Wildwood.

Vi decided to go to her room at nine o'clock. She wasn't especially tired, but she wanted to rise early the next morning

and accompany Enoch to the telegraph office. She had a feeling, just the smallest of inklings, that there might be something awaiting her there.

She went to Mrs. O'Flaherty's room to tell her friend of her plan. Mrs. O was seated at her dressing table. She wore a warm dressing gown of colorful flannel, and she was brushing her long hair, which was dark like Vi's but now streaked with silver.

"I hardly think Enoch needs help delivering our message," said Mrs. O'Flaherty with a sparkle in her sapphire blue eyes. "Is it possible you expect a telegram from someone? From, say, a certain professor of our acquaintance?"

Vi smiled and went to sit on Mrs. O'Flaherty's bed. From where she sat, she could see both her friend and herself in the dressing table mirror.

"It's possible," Vi said in a teasing way. "Oh, Mrs. O, I haven't had the chance to speak to you of anything but Mr. Clinch. Alma's fainting and then her confession and…well, that's taken all our energy. But when the professor was here, he and I talked, and, well…"

She paused. She knew what she wanted to say, but her heart was so full of emotion that she hardly knew where to begin.

Mrs. O'Flaherty helped her by asking, "Do you think he might send a telegram to inform you of his decision about living in India Bay?"

"Not yet," Vi replied. "He has probably just arrived in Boston, and he must talk with his children. He won't move unless he knows they want to come here."

"Is the children's approval all that stands in his way?" Mrs. O inquired. She laid her hairbrush aside and turned to face Vi.

Violet's Perplexing Puzzles

"There was another matter, but it is resolved now," Vi answered. She looked down for a few moments, then her head popped up, and she exclaimed, "He wanted *my* approval! He said he would come to India Bay only if I agreed. He asked if I would permit him to call on me."

"Call as in a courtship?" asked Mrs. O.

"He wouldn't use the word 'courtship.' But he means more than friendship. It's made me feel so strange, Mrs. O. All the time we were deciding what to do about Mr. Clinch and Alma, I was thinking about Mark — the professor — and I was happy inside, despite anything Mr. Clinch might be doing. I was thinking of Mark when I spoke up to Mr. Clinch, and it made me feel stronger."

Mrs. O'Flaherty smiled in an odd, sweet way, and she said, "It has been many years, but I remember those feelings, dear girl. Cherish them. Whatever comes, the love and affection in your heart is a wondrous gift. I hope you find a telegram tomorrow. But if not, trust that it will come soon. The professor isn't the kind of person who would trifle with your feelings."

Vi sighed. "I can't stop asking myself where this may all lead. Since the first night we spent in Samaritan House, when we found Tansy and Marigold, I have known that the work of helping people is right for me. Despite all we must do and all the problems we deal with, I am content with my life. Really content. I have admitted my — ah — special feelings for Mark Raymond to myself. And now it seems that he may feel the same. What will that do to my life, Mrs. O?"

"Turn it upside down, Vi girl."

Mrs. O came to sit beside Vi on the edge of the bed, and Vi laid her head on her friend's shoulder.

"I don't think I'm prepared to be turned upside down," Vi said. "It sounds like a dizzying prospect."

Mrs. O gently stroked Vi's hair and replied, "When love is new, it is dizzying and frustrating and perplexing. It is full of twists and turns that seem at times to spin your head. Yet it is filled with the promise of so much joy. No one is fully prepared, but you have always had a heart for adventure. I don't know if this love you feel now is the love of your life. But from what I have observed of the good professor, I believe you are in for a memorable adventure."

"We have many adventures ahead of us right here at Samaritan House," Vi said. She had not thought she was tired but found herself yawning lazily before she could continue. "Tansy and Marigold are returning at the end of the week. We must locate Alma's brother. We have to build the elevator, and I must find a way to help Miss Moran. We have to do something about getting fire service in Wildwood. And then there's Ed and Zoe."

"I think your brother and Zoe will resolve themselves without our help," Mrs. O'Flaherty laughed softly. "Before you do anything else, you must get some sleep. You've had a stressful day, though the results could not be better. Shall I say our prayers tonight?"

"Yes, please, Mrs. O," Vi replied. "I don't know why I am so sleepy all of a sudden."

" 'The sleep of a laborer is sweet,' " Mrs. O'Flaherty quoted from Ecclesiastes 5:12. "You've been laboring hard in the Lord's fields, Vi girl. Let's pray now and thank Him for the gift of rest."

Violet's Perplexing Puzzles

Near midnight—as Samaritan House lay still and all its residents slumbered peacefully—in an office several miles away, an overnight operator was writing down a message that was arriving in dots and dashes on his telegraph machine. He quickly translated the symbols into words, and since the message was not marked urgent, the operator slid the telegram into a box on his desk.

It would wait there, through the night. In the natural course of things, a boy would take it the next morning and deliver it to the home of the intended recipient. But things would not go exactly to form. Before the delivery boy could leave the office in downtown India Bay, the recipient herself would collect her telegram. And its contents would turn her life upside down.

Is Vi ready for a new dream?
Whose heart will harden against her?
Will her faith be strong enough?

Violet's story continues in:

VIOLET'S BUMPY RIDE

Book Six
of the
*A Life of Faith:
Violet Travilla* Series

A Life of Faith: Violet Travilla Series

MCP
Mission City Press

For more information, write to

Mission City Press at 202 Seond Ave. South,
Franklin, Tennessee 37064
or visit our Web Site at:

www.alifeoffaith.com

Collect all of our Elsie products!

A Life of Faith: Elsie Dinsmore Series

* Now Available as a Dramatized Audiobook!

Collect all of our Millie products!

A Life of Faith: Millie Keith Series

* Now Available as a Dramatized Audiobook!